Jerusalem Gap

by

t. r. pearson

Barking Mad Press

2010

For Kinch

I

I'd say I drive a Chevy pickup if it ran even half the
time. The linkage locks up. The coil shorts out. The
throttle body clots with sludge. I swap out pumps and
alternators like most people change their socks. I should
have sold the thing a few years back or driven it into a
pond, but I always think the next repair will be the one
to cure it. I don't know why. I'm not optimistic about
much of anything else.

So there I was sitting on the side of the road with
my bed stacked full of firewood. I was carrying it to a
woman in Afton, one of the Richmond horsy set who
weekends back in a hollow she insists on calling a glen. I
was a day late already from chainsaw trouble and had
promised I'd reach her by noon. That's why I didn't just
wait around for my Chevy to recover. I knew by the way
it had sputtered and quit it was having fuel pump spasms,
an electrical problem that reliably fixed itself once the
engine cooled off.

So I should have just raised the hood and sat in the
cab for half an hour, but somehow beating the
carburetor with a stick of kindling seemed therapeutic to
me at the time.

I was preoccupied, then, when a jalopy slowed up
beside me. It was a Nova coupe with muddy fender
skirts. I shot it a sly and sidelong glance, didn't want to
seem eager for help. Around here you get whiskery
layabouts who'll lean on your fender and prattle, offer to
carry you to the Cavalier Mart for a twenty dollar bill.

I heard a door hinge squeak and expected the worst,
but then the door swung shut again, and that Nova went
rumbling off in a cloud of incinerated oil.

They'd put her out on the pebbly shoulder, hard
beside the pavement. She was mostly collie by the looks
of her and maybe two months old. She was greasy and
matted and stank profoundly of cigarettes and the

barnyard, like a goat would smell if it lived on cow manure and Marlboro Lights.

She didn't show much interest in me. I showed precious little in her since a dog was about the last thing I wanted. I'd just gotten over a dog and had my ex-wife's cat already. Her new husband was allergic, and that cat had come in a package deal with a washing machine. It had seemed like a decent arrangement until the washer threw a bearing while the cat just kept on going.

He couldn't be bothered to kill a mouse, unspooled all my toilet paper. He swept my tabletops clean every chance he got and peed on my aspidistra. I would have set *him* out on the roadside if I'd been a touch more shiftless and less inclined to think a deal a deal.

Even still, I didn't guess I could leave a puppy where she'd get run over. I supposed once I'd dropped my load, I could swing by the Waynesboro pound. They could farm her out or put her down. I didn't much care which. That's what I told myself anyway as I snatched her up by her scruff and deposited her in the cab of my truck.

She was calm for a puppy. She lay sprawled on the seat looking at me with her head cocked and one of her ears flopped over. I troubled myself to inform her I had no use for a dog. She took the news well enough, yawned by way of reply. Then she laid her head on her forelegs and contemplated my dash.

She had a crusty eye and a drippy nostril. I could see each of her ribs. She was scuffed up along her near front shoulder and bald in a place or two like she'd come up on the short end of a scuffle. She nosed up a honey bun wrapper crammed in the bench seat crease and licked a little linty frosting from it.

"Lord, you stink," I told her as I turned the ignition key. The engine sputtered and caught, and I let it idle for a minute while I watched a flea hop off of her and straight over onto me.

She slept all the way to Afton, even rolled on her back for a bit and had a nap with her feet sticking up in the air. Then she stirred herself sufficiently to look out the window a little, and she even barked once we'd turned towards Swannanoa and a deer crossed the road just in front of us.

Right after she shot me a look I'd seen with a dog or two before, a glance that said, "I couldn't help myself. Don't hit me."

That told me all I needed to know about who she'd been turned out by, the sort of people who made a habit of kicking dogs around. I reached over and laid a hand to her head, lightly and without menace, and I suspect that's when it got unlikely we'd end up at the pound.

The horsy woman from Richmond I was hauling the firewood to had gone and named her glen Fair Valley. The iron sign by her driveway said as much. That seemed a little ambitious for a crease in the terrain where the sun probably found her for two hours a day and you had to look straight up to see the sky.

As I opened my door and rolled out of the cab, that puppy shoved me with her nose and came tumbling out behind me. She went on a full-scale tour of the lawn, had probably never seen grass before, certainly not fertilized and cultivated. I figured she'd come from the hard-packed dirt and weeds crowd out around Batesville. She'd certainly never seen whippets like the two cowering on the porch.

She looked at them, squatted and made her mark. They looked at her back and shivered. Those whippets had regal kennel-club names that I could never remember, and they moved around the property like waterbugs with fur.

For her part, that woman presently told me, "Aw," about my dog. She left the creature alone beyond that, didn't approach her or try to pet her. Just Aw as if to inform me, "You dropped a mongrel out of your truck."

She showed me where to stack the wood. She always showed me where to stack it, which was the same place I'd been stacking it for going on four years. Then she asked me, like she always did, if it was dry and seasoned. I assured her it was, which was true of maybe half of what I'd brought. I always piled the dry on top to give the other time to cure.

She burned it slowly and for show, just weekends in the fire place, and once I'd emptied the bed, I went in to lay a fire like I always did. Paper and kindling and fat wood and some stringy, split-out oak, fixed so it would just require a match to get it going.

She had one of those nineteenth century houses you find in this part of Virginia, with a slate roof and poplar siding chiseled to look like stone and mortar. A big square place, a four on four, improved with Richmond money.

Like always, she offered me a cocktail and, like always, I declined.

"Got to run her to the vet," I said of that puppy.

"Another time," that woman told me, the way she always did.

She had a husband back in Richmond who didn't like the country. She had a daughter in college out west somewhere and a son at a prep school up on Long Island. She owned a trio of thoroughbreds that seemed to conspire to be lame all the time and had a couple of women friends she saw in Charlottesville when she could bring herself to leave her glen for lunch.

I'd learned all of this while stacking wood over the past few years and feared the deeper intimacies hanging around for a drink might bring. Women have always talked to me. I don't exactly know why. I'm just another guy in a flannel shirt with a multi tool and ears.

"I'll call when I'm low," she told me, and I hoped she was talking firewood.

We looked out in the yard together to find that smelly mongrel puppy had herded both whippets up against a boxwood hedge. I whistled, not knowing what to expect, and that dog wheeled and came right to me. Those whippets, liberated, yodeled together and shivered and bounced.

That puppy tried to jump into the Chevy but was a bit too wee for it yet, so I grabbed her up and tossed her in, and off we went out of Fair Valley. Back into the proper afternoon. Under an open sky.

I drove west down towards Waynesboro and stopped at Homer's Grill. It used to be a Tastee Freeze

and is in the middle of nowhere much, out just beyond
town limits between a dairy farm and a nursery. I
ordered a couple of cheeseburgers. I carried them over
to the farthest table and brought the puppy out of the
truck to join me. This seemed a chance to both break
bread and lay out some stipulations. If I didn't want a
dog but was taking one regardless, there had to be a few
fast rules between us.

It's my practice of longstanding to talk to every
creature the same. Grown ups. Children. Cats. Dogs.
Livestock generally. I've even had a word or two with
timber rattlers in the woods. I'm all for trying to make
myself understood. So I broke up her burger and set her
wrapper on the ground. She went at it like she'd not seen
anything in the way of food for a while.

"Here's how it is," I told her. "I don't have the time
or patience to train you. You seem to ride all right, and
you know what a whippet's worth. So I'm thinking you'll
figure out what to do and what not to be about."

She left off licking her burger wrapper long enough
to look up at me. I took it as a sign she'd heard me and
was on board with the arrangement.

I'd decided by then to carry her to the clinic in
Stuart's Draft so Walter could check her out. I'd done a
little special work for Walter in a shed behind his house.
Walter played the cello. He'd come to it only lately, and
he couldn't manage much of anything that sounded
musical. Consequently, his wife had banished him and
his cello from the house, and Walter had decided to turn
his tool shed into a conservatory.

He needed space for a chair and a music stand and
then decided he wanted a toilet once his wife had let it be
known he wouldn't be tracking through her kitchen.

Walter's shed had been manufactured to look like a
miniature barn. He'd bought it at the lumberyard in
Staunton. It had a window in the back about the size of
an oven tray and particleboard on the walls and on the
floor. It clearly hadn't been designed with a powder
room in mind, and even with the mower and the
chainsaw out, the stink of gasoline was nearly
overwhelming.

We hung it with toilet deodorant blocks and let it sit open for a week.

Technically, I needed a permit to renovate Walter's shed and special dispensation to tap into the local sewer -- all paperwork and wasted time and fees. With Walter's approval, I cut a few corners and ignored an ordinance or two, so I got Walter up and sawing at his cello in a week. I even soundproofed that shed with an overabundance of Styrofoam insulation so Walter could massacre sonatas and nobody would hear a thing.

That's why I knew I could show up at the clinic in Stuart's Draft just out of the blue with a crusty, half-starved dog that needed a look. While his reception ladies might chafe, Walter had bonded with me over construction. I was confident he'd see me no matter what they said.

I was obliged to use a tie down from the truck bed for a leash. The waiting room was full of lap dogs, an assortment of spaniels and terriers and poodles. They were cowering from the pair of cats who had free run of the place. One of them was old and half-blind. He slept on a towel on top of the counter and would take a swat if you gave him the chance while you were paying your bill.

The other was monstrously large for a cat and liked to put dogs in their place. His name was Brady, and he was a twenty pounder at least. He did regular waiting-room rounds to see who was ripe for intimidation. It was the rare dog that would take on Brady. Some of those country short hairs would have a go with the barking and the spittle and the bouncing all around until Brady closed on them and gave them a tap with his claws.

Most dogs had the sense to shrink and submit and peer timidly at Brady as if to tell him, "I know you're a cat and all, but *Hey.*"

Of course, he swatted them too but mostly in the way of easy sport.

My puppy was stretched out on the floor, and she didn't even stir when Brady came over. If it had been me, I'd have been retreating as far as that tie down would allow. But that puppy didn't twitch, which caused me to wonder if she was sick and feverish. I all but gave her distemper on the spot. I flashed on all the potential puppy trouble I'd be spared if all Walter could do was diagnose her, shake his head, and put her down. I didn't know her well enough to be acutely sad about it, but I knew me well enough to feel relieved.

Brady got right up on her, three inches from her nose. He even crouched and let his mouth sag open while he took her fragrance in. She never moved. She just watched him at the end of her crusty snout in a lazy way that suggested she'd seen bigger cats already. He didn't even smack her but finally only wheeled and walked away.

A reception lady, the one with the elaborate pile of hair, told Walter over the intercom, "Donald Atwell's here. He's not in the book." She said it like I was barely evolved and upright.

Walter, of course, stepped right out and told me, "Come on back."

Walter was partners in the clinic with a lady vet who let him come and go as he pleased. He was crowding sixty and didn't make farm calls anymore. Walter was chiefly cats and dogs three days a week and Bach in the tool shed the rest of the time. I'd met him when I'd brought in my ex-wife's cat, back before I knew cat vomit was a regular cat thing.

When I'd climbed from my truck in the parking lot, I'd seen him out in the pasture beside the clinic. He'd had his arm up to the shoulder in the back end of a cow. He was feeling for something, looked like a man groping for his car keys, and I wandered over with my cat carrier in hand and said to Walter, "Hey."

"How you?"

"All right."

"She's stopped up," he told me, tossing his head towards the cow.

"I guess you'd better hope so."

"What you got?"

"Cat."

"Down with something?"

"Throws up a lot."

"They'll do that," Walter told me and removed his arm with a slurpy pop.

Walter's vet uniform is a black knit shirt that's always covered in hair and ragged khakis he's usually wiped God knows what all over. He hardly looks like a man who'd pass his down time trying to play the cello.

"Wow," he said once I'd walked my puppy into the examination room. "She smells like a Frogtown Friday night."

I told him how she'd come to me as he looked her over, and I invited him to find something bad wrong with her so I wouldn't have to carry her home. He took her temperature. He eyed her all over and felt around with his hands. She sat there and endured it, even once Walter had broken out the needles and had started giving her all the shots we were sure she'd never had.

"She got a name?"

"I'm thinking Nova," I told him. "They put her out of one."

"Lot of collie in her. You'll need to break her from herding every darn thing."

"So she's fine?"

"Put this in her runny eye." He gave me a tube of ointment. "And wash her in this," he told me as he handed me a bottle of flea shampoo. Walter ruffled her fur to show me her skin. She was colonized with fleas. "Maybe twice today and once tomorrow. Bring her back in a month."

"How's the cello?" I asked Walter as I was reaching for the doorknob.

Walter exhaled and shook his head. "Slow," he told me. "Got no frets."

"You knew that going in, right?"

Walter shrugged and nodded.

I don't suppose I'll ever forget the look on Walter's face once I'd finished off his conservatory. He was sitting right there in the middle of it sawing on his cello, trying out the acoustics, settling into his folding chair. His music, such as it was, bordered on unholy racket. It was flat and screechy and doggedly untuneful, but Walter was smiling anyway. Swaying with his eyes shut. I'd never seen a man look more content.

"Love her, why don't you," Walter suggested as I swung open the examination room door. "Looks like you'll be the first."

II

I left her out in the yard while I went in and had a word with the cat. He was asleep in his chair. It was my chair really, the one I used to read in before Pom Pom came into my home to drive me to the couch. That's right. Pom Pom. My ex-wife did that. I've never known occasion to call him anything but, "HEY!"

So I went in the house and woke him up, told him what was outside. As long as we were chatting, I recommended the litter box over the aspidistra. Then I stepped out after the puppy who was chewing on a stick. She followed me in, and Nova and the cat had their inaugural encounter. The cat got shirty and put out. The dog just sat and watched. Cat hackles went up. There was about a quarter hour of hissing. The puppy stretched out on the throw rug underneath the coffee table and suffered herself to be circled and sniffed until the fleas began to migrate when Pom Pom retired to the back room to leave a few on my bed.

I bathed Nova in a cooler I rarely got much use from. She took it like a dog who was weary of smelling of cow flop and Marlboro Lights. She groaned with pleasure when I soaped her up. When I rinsed her. When I repeated. Then I drained the nasty water and covered the cooler with a towel so she could shake. When I snatched it off, I discovered her fleas had all gone Kamikaze. They were bailing onto anything at hand.

I fed her leftover chicken nuggets and the kibble the cat hadn't eaten. She seemed reluctant at first to drink water that wasn't stagnating in a trough, but she warmed to the good stuff soon enough and polished off about a quart. Then I took her outside, and she peed and rolled around a bit on the lawn before she followed me back into the house and collapsed on the floor.

I used to have a regular job at a building supply
store in the valley. I talked on the phone all day and
pieced together wholesale orders, knew just about every
contractor from Raphine to Weyers Cave. I had a wife
and a mortgage and two car payments. We had suburban
neighbors we socialized with and even sort of knew --
like you know your mailman, your banker, or your
barber. We went down to Southern Shores once a year
because my wife had always gone to Southern Shores.
We opened presents on Christmas Eve because she'd
been raised to do it that way. We attended the Baptist
church in Staunton because that's where her people had
always worshipped.

By the time she met the fellow who would become
her second husband, I was ready to let somebody else do
what she wanted for a while. I could tell by the way she
talked about him all I needed to get was gone. She was
the one who insisted I move out of the valley. If I hung
around, I'd serve as handy proof she'd been divorced,
and she came from people who stayed married for good
and all no matter what.

It worked out well enough for me. I took a house
near Greenwood on a sizable estate where I don't pay
rent and earn a stipend for general maintenance work.
I'm allowed to cut all the wood I like and sell it off for
pocket money. The folks who own the place live in
Dallas and only make it to Virginia for two weeks in
August and maybe a half dozen weekends the rest of the
year. They bought that farm with hedge fund money
and have another estate or three.

I mow the yard. I make repairs. I paint the plank
fencing when nothing else needs doing. I cut lap wood
off the property and sell it by the cord. I hike the trails.
I read fat books. I tinker with my pickup. I stop in at the
post office maybe twice a week where the girl who sorts
and carries the mail is always quick to tell me that my
neighbors, without exception, think I'm odd.

That pleases me the way being a Baptist in Staunton
never would.

Once Nova was up and dry enough, I took her out
to see the cattle. A guy from down by Nellysford leases

the pasture and keeps maybe eighty head of belted
Galloways on the estate throughout the year. He's a
funny old coot. I can only understand about every other
word he says. Half the problem is Red Man plug chew
and the rest is his Nelson County roots.

Beyond that, it doesn't help that he's excited all the
time. He'll start in about the weather or the government
in D.C. or stock car qualifying on the oval down in
Martinsville, and I'll have just enough occasion to get the
lay of the terrain before he lapses into high velocity
backwoods yokelese.

He can go on for a quarter hour without me doing a
thing but nodding. He might as well be speaking Urdu
for the good it does me to listen. I'll usually give him his
head for a while and then find a gap to tell him, "Well,"
before I wheel around and wander off like I have
somewhere else to be.

He never cares. He's partial to cows. They hear his
truck and come running. They bellow and moo and
close around him like disciples, even when he doesn't
have a round bale with him or a mineral lick to toss onto
the ground.

I didn't want Nova herding them. Once a dog starts
chasing cows, it's a hard thing to break and discourage.
So I led her up the main drive and through the pasture
gate. She came along fine, didn't seem the sort of canine
to get distracted.

The herd was gathered on the rise just east of the
main house. It was a grand old place, a touch finer than
Fair Valley in the glen. A Federalist monstrosity with
porches all over and a half dozen chimneys throughout.
The slate roof was new. The paint was fresh. The
windows and doors had all been retooled and refitted by
a team of artisans brought down from a museum in
Chicago. The flooring was mostly wormy heart pine,
planks about ten inches wide. A fellow had come clean
from Belfast to repair the plaster.

All this for a house that saw its owners maybe three
weeks a year. Those folks were decent enough, and
didn't need their cow man complaining about my dog, so

breaking her herding instinct was some serious business for me.

She was too low to see the cattle until we'd gained the hilltop, and when the herd came into view, the sight of it stopped her cold. They did that thing cows do -- swung their massive heads around, looked at us, lowed a little, and peed.

Nova whimpered and shivered like a whippet might, but that was about as far as her upset went. She just stayed where she was and watched the cows. There were a few dozen calves among them, and they charged at us the way calves will and danced around the hillside. Even then, Nova only sat and watched. I could tell by the way she played her gaze from one edge of the herd to the other that she was fully occupied with collie geometry.

The cow man had dogs he culled the herd with, and they were something to see in action. Australian shepherds with what looked a dash of foxhound each. They rode in the truck bed and hopped out once that fellow had stopped in the pasture. He hadn't worked up elaborate signals to tell them what to do. They knew their job was to split the herd in three or four different parcels and then go on dividing whatever portion their master pointed at. It was simple and pure, a pleasure to watch because they did geometry too.

They'd sit there the two of them, side by side, and study the cows for a minute while the cattle, torn between greeting their owner and avoiding his herding dogs, would dither and moo and pee, of course, and end up doing nothing.

That fellow, for his part, would say just, "All right," and off those dogs would go on whatever route they'd settled on to split the herd to best effect. They'd take off at tangents, swing wide, divide up and swing wider still. The cattle would close in and clump together. They'd watch those dogs and bellow out the bovine version of "Oh, hell."

By now the cow man usually wasn't paying any attention. If I was around to watch, he was already bathing me in prattle by then. The dogs didn't need him. They'd done their math, and once they'd looped behind the cows, one of them would sweep down for the incision. He'd blast right in and cut the herd cleanly in half, send two clumps of cattle thundering in different directions. Then those dogs would circle a half herd and drive it to one side before slicing through and dividing it neatly in two. They'd do the same to the other half if the cow man needed it done.

He'd whistle and point at the portion he wanted, and those dogs would ring it round. They'd drive it across the pasture towards the corral. That cow man would usually be carping to me about the droughty weather or something by then. At length he'd wander over to shut the gate. He had no need to hurry. His dogs would stand at the opening and keep the cows in until he arrived.

Once he'd told them, "Go on," they'd race across the pasture and jump into the bed of his truck.

I'd tried to be friendly with them a time or two, love them up a little, but they couldn't keep their eyes off all the cattle they hadn't herded yet.

While Nova might have been a herding dog by instinct and disposition, I didn't want her devoted to it for a couple of reasons at once. Nothing good can come of running cattle in a recreational sort of way. They're too big and dumb and clumsy to get chased through a field for no reason, can get broken down in an instant by a dog out on a spree. Moreover, I didn't want Nova thinking pushing cows was her job. I didn't want her fixed on herding math the way the cow man's shepherds were.

To that end, I let her study the herd on our first trip into the pasture, allowed her to even do her fledgling collie herding math before I leaned down and gave her a firm nudge. I poked her once with my finger and told her, "No, ma'am." It was a thing, I'd decided, the two of us would make time for every day until I was convinced she could see a cow and not feel the need to drive it.

We walked out of the pasture the way we'd come in, and I did my usual circuit of the big house, testing all the doorknobs and checking all the windows a potential thief might try. Then we had a look out at the barn where the equipment was where I'd left it, and we continued into the woods on the walk I usually take. I doubted she was up to the entire trek, so we only followed the trail up to the ridge line. We flushed a few deer along the way, and Nova took an interest in them. Finally up on the flat, we surprised two does, and that's when I told her, "Go!"

They were the anti-cow. She'd never herd one and she'd never hurt one either. She just needed my permission to tear at them at full puppy speed. She chased them out of sight. I could hear her yelping, and then she came dragging back to me once I'd whistled for her twice. She plopped down right in the middle of the trail, her tongue flopped out on the side. She looked up at me, panting, in a way I took to mean, "I've had as full a day as I can stand."

We went down the way we'd come and walked the driveway towards our house. I was carrying her well before we'd reached the yard.

I'd decided by then Carl wouldn't mind if this new girl slept on his bed. Carl had been a hard case, ill-natured and opinionated. He never got along with anybody but me, and the two of us quarreled routinely. I have my ways. Carl had his, and most everything we undertook was cause for negotiation.

Carl was sort of a retriever. Not a proper, pedigreed dog. I met his mother once. She looked like she was maybe a quarter setter while his father had been a chocolate lab his owners turned out nights to prowl. Carl had belonged to one of our neighbors over in the suburbs. They were the sort of people who shouldn't have had either children or a dog, so they had three of the former and two of the latter and neglected the whole assortment. The kids were savages. One of the dogs -- I think his name was Roscoe -- got hauled off by a coyote for a snack.

As far as I could tell, Carl was the only adult in the family. The parents, Dale and Judy, had been high school sweethearts and had never between them bothered to grow up. They were always off at concerts or junkets to Atlantic City, went to Honolulu once and left the children all at home. The oldest one was eleven, and she

was too much like her mother to take any sort of sisterly
interest in the other two. They ran wild for a day. I
remember rolling home from work and seeing the
younger ones playing naked in the yard.

My wife found it unseemly to live in a place where
folks would abandon their children to go off to Hawaii
and pretend to shop for time-share real estate.

"We've got to do something," she said, by which, of
course, she meant me.

I ended up moving in to Dale and Judy's for what
turned out to be five days. I didn't really get beyond
putting trousers on the children. They were too far gone
to have any use for anything I told them. We ate Hungry
Man dinners that their parents had left them, and I
locked them in at night and turned them out come
morning. I took time off from work to sit and watch
them break everything in their yard.

That's when I got to know Carl. He had a way
about him like no dog I'd ever come across before. I'd
say he was expressive, but that doesn't quite cover it.
Carl was more singularly himself than any human I've
ever known. He had habits and quirks and ethics even.
And Lord did he have opinions.

At first I thought it was gas. Me and Carl were in
the carport overseeing a spot of demolition. All three of
those kids were bringing down the lamppost by the walk,
and once they'd forced the pole to bend and were riding
it to the ground, Carl uncorked a spot of commentary.
It wasn't a growl exactly, more in the way of throaty
grumble. The kind of racket any crotchety onlooker
would have made.

It was easy enough to translate. "Would you look at
that?"

"I know," I said, and Carl dropped his heavy head to
the slab with a huff.

Those kids got up to something else thereafter, and
Carl disapproved again. I studied him hard, had to
wonder if somebody's uncle was in there. He rolled his
eyes up at me and grumbled another time.

"Fig Newton?" I offered. I had a half-empty sleeve.
Carl told me in his fashion, "I guess."

Carl was enough to make a heathen like me believe in reincarnation. Right and wrong for most dogs takes the form of do your business in the yard and don't eat the cat, but Carl lived in a moral universe. He had a feel for shades of gray. Of course, nobody noticed it but me. You had to pay a little attention.

When Dale and Judy finally came home, Carl was the first one to let them have it. He lumbered down to the end of the driveway as they were pulling in, rolling up in Dale's new Impala (he always had a new one) with Judy waving her bronze hand and lacquered nails at the kids.

Carl barked with menace to tell Dale and Judy what rubbish he found them to be. They didn't hear him, of course, not the way he'd meant to be heard. They'd noticed me by then, and Dale rolled out of his sedan and said exactly what I knew he'd say.

"What?!"

In Dale's mind he was always blameless just like he was always dapper and witty.

I walked up to Dale and slugged him, which I knew Carl couldn't do.

They moved away not three weeks later. Dale had talked himself into a job somewhere, and they had one of those yard sales that irked my ex-wife to no end -- just dragged all their crap out onto the lawn, and people swarmed like flies. They pulled out on a Thursday in Dale's Impala hauling a little trailer.

I found Carl tied to a clothesline pole in Dale and Judy's back yard.

I was already my ex's future former husband by then, so it hardly mattered that she didn't care for Carl or want him in the house. Being in that house, as far as I could tell, wasn't in the cards for either of us for much longer.

Carl, as it turned out, was born to live on an estate. Those folks in Dallas might have bought the place, but it was Carl's from end to end. He paraded around the property. There was nowhere he didn't go, and when we argued -- and me and Carl had our share of pitched disagreements -- he'd retire to the porch of the main house and live there for a while.

My feelings for Carl were complicated. I was only with him for his last four years, so he was well beyond training. All I had to do was tolerate him. He wasn't the sort of creature I could feel protective of. We lived together like a pair of cantankerous bachelors, having walks on occasion and ongoing spats and being in each other's way. Then one night Carl did me the only favor I'd ever known him to do. He did me the courtesy of dying in his sleep.

I'd never carried him to the vet. I'd never taken him anywhere once I'd hauled him over Afton Mountain and onto his estate. So I don't know what was wrong with him, can't even say how old he was. I like to think Carl had simply had enough.

I got the backhoe out of the barn and dug him a proper grave in the pasture. He ended up having the sort of send off that would have pleased even him. There were four of us at the graveside -- me and Agatha, who cleans the house, and the boys who stop by weekly to change the flowers. Apparently, hedge fund money will buy you a maid for a mansion you're hardly ever in and a contract with a florist to keep it prettied up and fragrant. All that mattered to me was they'd all known Carl and had taken him as he was.

Agatha is from Anguilla, and she has a graceful way about her. She's quick to laugh and sing and is kinder than people around here tend to be. She sang a hymm in her high, sweet voice. Even the cows wandered over to listen. Billy, the shorter of the boys and the gayer of the two, cried so hard he had to fight for breath. The other one, Ben, told Billy Carl wouldn't have wanted us to cry.

I'm sure he was right, but it didn't stop me. They'd all wandered off by then, and there I sat, with an audience of banded Galloways, bawling on the backhoe.

I cleaned up Carl's things and packed them all away. Laundered his bed. Washed his dishes. Threw out his smelly rope chew. Then I led a life of talking to a dead dog for about three months. I couldn't help myself. The

cat wasn't about to take any interest in me. Carl had been
gone a little over a year when Nova got put out.

I set Carl's rubber placemat back on the kitchen
floor. His bed went back in his spot between the brass
lamp and the rocker, and Nova was on it, sniffing, as
soon as I'd laid it down.

When I woke up in the small hours, she was beside
me on the bed. Asleep on her back with her feet in the
air -- at full ease and secure. I rubbed her belly. She
whimpered and rolled, and I started to feel a little whole.

III

Nova committed the usual puppy transgressions, but I can hardly remember them now. Chewed on a chair leg. Dug a few holes in the yard. Threw up a chipmunk on the sofa. She had a bubbly spirit, was never grumpy like Carl. Nova always tolerated the advice I gave her with a smile, the sort of grin that said to me, "I hear you." Then she'd do whatever she'd do.

It turned out, I didn't have to worry about her giving chase to the cattle. She was happy enough to run after deer by way of recreation, but what she really loved was people, anywhere and anyhow. Ordinarily, that wasn't a problem for me, since there weren't many people around. Nobody came onto the property, as a rule, who wasn't supposed to be here. But when I carried her with me out in the world, she had a way of flagging folks down.

That was sort of a problem for me because I'm not, in truth, a people person. Agatha calls me Mr. Prickly, and I guess it probably suits. My experience with people generally is that they're just not worth the trouble. Carl was of the same opinion, so he never tempted strangers to come over and tell us, "Hey." Out in the world, Carl and me would give the stink eye together.

Nova had a bigger heart and was indiscriminate with her affection. I'm sure she loved me most, when it came down to it, but she went ahead and liked everybody else. I found out about her weakness a month after I'd brought her home. She was at that gangly age when she was more awkward than cute. Her coat was all cowlicks. Her legs were too long, and her ears looked too big for her head. She was lacking, consequently, in puppy magnetism, so I guessed I could carry her into town and nobody would make a fuss.

I went to the hardware store in Crozet, in the little square there by the depot, and I let her out to make her business before I went in to buy some screws. She was on Carl's leash, and we'd been working a few weeks on her etiquette.

I'd informed her I liked a dog who could walk quietly at my side, not just back on the farm but out in the world when walking was called for. As I recall, she'd glanced my way as if to tell me, "Wouldn't that be nice."

So she was pulling and prancing and altogether delighted to be out in town when she caught sight of a woman coming out of the pharmacy. A square woman in a warm-up suit with unnaturally highlit hair.

Nova stamped with doggy excitement and grinned at that woman. She managed to cast a spell upon her. I heard the woman say, "Aw," as she struck out towards us, came straight across the lot.

"Your dog's smiling at me," was the only thing she bothered to say to me. Then she held an extended confab with the puppy.

She told Nova about a dog she'd had, some sort of hound she'd loved to pieces. This went on for a quarter hour, and I had screws to buy. She finally left us alone after Nova had kept her around with a couple of whimpers, and once that woman had climbed into her LeSabre and driven into the road, I told Nova, "You can't be smiling at everybody, especially people we don't know. I'll never take you anywhere. I'll leave you at the house."

She glanced up at me and grinned -- Nova's way of saying, "I hear you."

Agatha was somebody I wanted her to meet, wanted her to like the way I liked her. She was a beautiful, coffee-colored woman with an island accent, given to spangly jewelry and quick to laugh. I saw her twice a month. She came every other Thursday morning to tidy up the house, and I had to let her in because I had the only key. Not actually but effectively. I'd made a key for Agatha, but she wouldn't ever use it because the people who owned the place hadn't seen fit to trust her with one themselves.

They were funny that way. I went for a while thinking they were suspicious of people, but it finally dawned on me that, if something went wrong, they wanted just me to blame. Agatha seemed to know that before I'd figured it out, and she wouldn't go into the house unless I was with her.

She made a fuss over Nova when I introduced them. "Oh, Mr. Prickly," she told me. "She's so happy."

"Yeah," I said with the sort of grumble that caused Agatha to laugh.

"Whatever will we do, Mr. Prickly," she said, "if she makes you happy too?"

Then Agatha told me about a dream she'd had. She was always telling me about her dreams, and they weren't the sort of dreams most people feel a burning need to speak of. Arriving at Dulles airport stupendously underdressed. Having breakfast in a diner with the Pope. The sort of thing nobody really ever wants to hear about. Agatha's dreams were of a different stripe. Mysterious and strange.

"I was in the forest," she told me. "This forest." We were standing in the kitchen of the big house at the time, and she swept her arm before her to take in the whole Blue Ridge. "June light," she told me, "when the leaves are finally out and the sun can barely break through. Like being on the bottom of the sea."

She wiped the marble countertop as she spoke. It was spotless, of course, already, but Agatha got paid to clean. She never just made a show of it. The house might have been immaculate when she stepped inside, but she always went at it like it was crying out for a tidy up.

"I was on a path. Just me. But wider, like a road. And walking down, down, towards that river," and she pointed vaguely west.

"The Moorman River?" I asked her. It snaked through the adjacent valley.

Agatha nodded. "And there were people in the woods."

"People?"

"Men. Women. Children. White. Brown. Black. And they are standing. Just standing. Not on the path with me, but off in the woods. And I say to them, 'What is this place?' but they tell me nothing. I am there, but I am not there. They see me, but they don't. It is a beautiful, strange dream. I'm frightened. I am comforted."

All the while, Nova had been sitting on the kitchen floor at my feet. Watching Agatha. Favoring her with a doggy grin.

"I walk down, down to the water, and who do I see?" She asked it of Nova more than she asked it of me. "Carl," she said. "He is happy. Happy anyway for Carl."

She put her hand beneath Nova's snout and lifted the puppy's head. Nova looked almost hypnotized as Agatha gazed into her eyes. "And do you know what I told him? Do you?" The puppy didn't seem to. I doubted I did either.

"The thing I never got to say. I finally told Carl goodbye."

Nova whimpered a little and stamped her feet as Agatha leaned low to kiss her on the snout. "Hello," she said. "Goodbye," she said.

With that she cleaned the spotless kitchen. Reshined the silver. Waxed the dining room table. Vacuumed the library rug. For my part, I made my rounds checking on the mousetraps I'd put out. If there was anything to clean up from visit to visit, it was a peppering of mouse droppings. I baited my traps with peanut butter and caught the foolish ones, but a relentless few of them laid siege to the pantry in a regular sort of way and got into the rice and pasta.

I had help in the warmer months from a black snake I called Howard because he was scarred and scuffed up and stunted like a Howard I had known. I'd met him a couple years back when I was doing a little plumbing. One of my vermin friends had chewed through a water line out in the mudroom and I was having to cut a hole in the wall to get at the thing and mend it.

So there Carl and I were in the mudroom cutting a hole in perfectly good drywall, and who do we find in the insulation but all fourteen inches of Howard. Since he'd heard us coming, he didn't look surprised, but I have to say that Carl and I weren't really expecting him. Carl barked. I lurched back and banged into the coat tree. Howard stayed exactly where he'd been and gave us occasion to calm down.

This part of the world is infested with snakes. We're mindful mostly of rattlers because they're toxic and aggressive and all over the stinking place. The copperheads come out at night when the rattlesnakes are sleeping, and if you dodge those two there's a wealth of serpents that'll just give you tetanus and a fright. I imagine the bulk of blacksnakes would as soon bite you as not, but Howard turned out to be a live-and-let-live sort of serpent. Unless, of course, you happened to be a mouse.

He seemed almost happy to see me because his insulation was damp. Howard didn't want that leak any more than I did. He was close to the piece of pipe the mouse had chewed a hole in, and I didn't want to stick my hand in the wall and come out with a snake bite. But it looked to me like he was just waiting around for me to see to his bit of bother. So I reached in and cut the bad pipe out, and Howard appeared to approve.

I took proper leave of Howard before I walled him in again. "You get them in there," I said to him. "I'll try to catch them out here."

On those Thursdays when Agatha cleans, Ben and Billy change out the flowers. There's a huge vase fixed to the bannister post right in the middle of the grand front foyer, and those boys are paid to keep it showy on a fitting scale. So once they've rolled up in their van, I haul the old arrangement to the compost pile, and Ben and Billy spend an hour or more refilling that vase afresh.

The ceiling is thirty feet overhead, so they can build as high as they dare to, and they must be paid well for their trouble since they go massive most of the time. They're gifted, those two. I hardly know anything about flower arranging, but like most people I can tell the difference between floral beauty and chaff.

Those boys had a little shop for a while out west of Charlottesville in Ivy, but the clientele they cultivated didn't want to come to the store. They required that Ben and Billy service their cosmetic horse farms, their renovated manor houses, their faux Jeffersonian estates. At length they traded their store for an Econoline and a greenhouse, and now they drive around changing out arrangements all over the countryside.

We have lunch together, the four of us, every other week. Agatha told the boys about her dream over a spicy island stew she'd thrown together the night before. She had an aunt who kept her in Rockfield Pepper Sauce, an Anguillan staple, and she sloshed it in just about everything she cooked. It made Tabasco seem like a cereal topping. The Rockfield was treacherous to eat, so there me and boys sat eating stew and sweating over each spoonful while Agatha told us about those people standing in the woods and Carl down at the bottom waiting for her by the water.

Ben was the sort who liked to tease the deeper meaning out of things. There were no innocent remarks, in Ben's view, or incoherent dreams. Everything had a buried logic if you were willing to work it out. "What do you mean by that?" was Ben's favorite question, even if you'd only told him, "Good morning."

Agatha's dream was child's play for Ben.

"Where were you?" he asked.

"In the forest."

"Yes, but where?"

"There," she said and pointed towards the refrigerator. From where we were sitting that made it just a little west of north. "Near that river," she told Ben and looked at me.

"The Moorman," I said, but Ben was onto just the spot she'd dreamed about already.

"We know that place," he told us.

"We do?" Billy said.

Ben nodded and describe a crease in the terrain where he and Billy gathered laurel and Canadian violet, pink lady's slipper and wild azalea.

"Oh." Billy recalled it all at once. "With all the graves in the woods."

Agatha gasped. She has a weakness for spirits and haunts and ghostly premonitions. A graveyard can leave her faint and quivering even at high noon. She's in precisely the wrong spot for that manner of affliction since, in this part of Virginia, people are buried all over the place.

There were a half dozen people buried on the very estate where we were sitting, not in any sort of proper cemetery but just out behind the ice house in a grove of tulip trees. A couple of them had real headstones that the weather had all but erased, but the rest were just marked by upended rocks and six feet of sunken terrain. I can't think of anywhere else I've ever lived, or passed through really with attention, where people were planted in most any spot a guy with a shovel had pleased.

I'd stumbled across graveyards all over the woods. They were usually overgrown with forest underlay -- black coho and wild ferns, the odd sticker thicket. There was one I walked past most every day up at the border of the estate where the property joined the National Park.

It was kept up by a boy whose father would oversee the work. I had run across them a time or two while they were tidying up the place. They both lived in the Shenandoah Valley, but the father's people had come from up on the ridge, and that gentleman told me about the burials he'd attended as a child. I recall him pointing to a rock that his uncle had been laid under and another one just beside it where they'd put his aunt in time. It seemed the family had owned a house nearby, a cabin anyway, which the forest had reclaimed the way the forest will.

That fellow was keen to keep the graveyard up so his people could always find it. His son was more the sort who just wanted to cut the weeds and go home.

You could hike right by that graveyard and not even notice it was there. Just gray rocks that had come to hand, standing up on end. It all looked haphazard and accidental. I found the thought of such places melancholy, and I never passed that spot without a twinge over how little everything comes to in the end.

"Tell me your dream," Ben charged Agatha. "Right from the beginning."

Agatha acquainted us with the trail she'd been on and the pitch of serenity she'd felt in the woods. For me, that was the part of the story that was most profoundly dreamlike. I'd taken Agatha on a walk once on a fine spring afternoon, and even the squirrels in the hickory trees had managed to unnerve her. She had her snake fear and her bear fear and her opossum and raccoon fear, which were separate and apart from her upset over spirits in the woods.

"The people," Ben asked her. "Were they kind of halfway down?"

That seemed about right to Agatha who nodded.

"Both sides of the trail?"

She nodded again.

And Ben's next words were, "Stop it!"

They were directed at Billy who was feeding saltines to Nova. He wasn't doing it to make a friend. She loved everybody already. She would have been sitting there smiling at Billy if he'd given her crackers or not. He offered her saltines because, in Ben's view, Billy was an over feeder. They owned a terrier named Poughkeepsie Billy had crackered half to death. She looked like she'd been plugged into a compressor and inflated.

"Just one more," Billy pleaded. It's what he always said. Carl used to get an entire sleeve of saltines every other week.

So Agatha's dream was forestalled by one of Ben and Billy's quarrels. They were always trying to strike a balance between Ben's sober sense of duty and Billy's open-hearted lavishness. In this case it ended up with two additional saltines before Billy handed the sleeve to Ben who shut it up in the cracker box.

"Now," Ben said to Agatha, "so the people were halfway down?"

She nodded.

"And the trail was like a fire road, wide and weedy, wasn't it?"

That was a touch too eerily specific for Agatha, who laid her hand to her sternum the way she usually did when she was shaken up.

"That's it," Ben told her. "Jerusalem Gap."

Now I'd been in the general area for years by then and had hiked all over the countryside for probably a couple of decades. I liked to think I was conversant in the local mountain landmarks, but that was the first time I'd ever so much as heard of Jerusalem Gap.

"You mean Turk's Gap, don't you?" I said to Ben.

He told me that he didn't.

"South of Pond Ridge?" I asked him.

He nodded.

"North of Beagle Gap and Bear Den?"

Ben nodded again.

"Which fire road?"

Ben rose from his stool at the kitchen island and went out to his van. He came back with a gazetteer just like the one I had at home. The book flopped open to the local Albemarle County map.

"We're here," Ben said and pointed. The scale was such that even our private estate road was marked on the page. "Jerusalem Gap," he told me and touched a blank spot in the forest up in the park proper, a little north of west. The topographical lines laid upon it made it look like nothing much. It wasn't identified as any sort of gap or hollow at all.

"Who told you what it was called?" I asked him, and Ben glanced at Billy for a consult.

"That woman in Keswick, wasn't it?" Billy said. "Polishing the silver in that big yellow Georgian place with all those fake library books."

"Right," Ben said. "What was her name?"

"Delfinia or Philadelphia or something."

"We'd brought in a bunch of laurel that we'd hauled out of the park," Ben said. "She asked us where from, and we described it. She called it Jerusalem Gap. Said she had a sister or cousin or something buried there. Right?"

Billy fed Nova his last saltine and nodded.

I studied the gazetteer laid out on the granite counter and finally said, "Don't think I've been down through here, and I've been all over the place."

Ben told me how to reach it. You had to wander off the trail. The fire road hadn't been kept up for years and ended at a washout, so you needed to bushwhack a little to find the way.

I helped the boys pack up the van. Then I collected all the mice I'd killed and carried them in a bucket out to the pasture where I buried them in a hole. Agatha finished her tidying up, and I locked the house behind us, walked her out to her Nissan that I'd doctored on more than once.

Agatha bent low to say another goodbye to Nova. After her Carl dream, she was newly mindful of goodbyes.

Me and Nova went for a walk before returning home. Nova studied the cows as we crossed a corner of the pasture, but she didn't give chase. She saved that for the deer in the woods, just like I had encouraged, and she made it all the way down the ridge line without wearing out.

It was coming on November so we didn't have to worry about rattlers. To see Nova taking in the smells and chasing squirrels for sport, I was reacquainted with just the sort of pleasure a dog can bring. Carl was so ill-natured and grumpy, he'd not been built to be much of a pal, but Nova would sweep out from me on a circuit through the woods and then race back to poke me with her pointed collie snout. She'd smile up at me with her white needle teeth, her way of telling me, "Hi!" Then off she'd go again on a loop, racing with her nose down.

That was the afternoon I finally fell in love with Nova. It isn't the sort of thing that's guaranteed between me and a dog. I admired and respected Carl, but I can't say that I loved him, and I had a dog named Duke a few decades back that I didn't consistently like. It happens or it doesn't, and it happened for me with Nova. I even remember the moment when it did.

She'd chased a doe up over a hummock of ground and out of sight. She'd gone hell for leather in full collie yodel and then came rambling back. She jogged into view up over the rise. I saw her, and she saw me. Nova smiled. I could tell from even back where I was, and she changed gears and dashed my way. She ran to me as hard as she could manage. She poked me with her snout. She whirled around and poked me again like we'd been separated for ages. She barked and reared to lay her freckled front paws on my thigh, just the sort of thing I'd ordinarily discourage.

That's when I did my math. I guessed I could count on a dozen years with her, maybe even more if she was a hardy creature and I was lucky. And I managed somehow in my head to make a dozen years seem like enough.

IV

The owners flew in from Dallas for a long weekend in March. They had their own jet and their own full-time pilot, two dogs that traveled with them virtually everywhere they went, along with a chef who accompanied them most occasions.

My boss insisted I call him Michael. His wife preferred Mrs. McShane. Michael liked to work on projects, especially improvements around the house. Beyond leveraging investments and levying fees, he didn't seem to have any skills that I could make productive use of. Michael would decide the powder room could use an outlet or the back veranda could stand to have a wet bar, and he'd just flail away at whatever needed to be destroyed. Michael had an urge for demolition, but that was as far as his urges went. It usually took me a day or two after he'd left to finally set everything right.

I liked him well enough because he was decent as far as it went. Mrs. McShane was the brittle one. She and the chef together had sort of a vodka problem. They palled around in the kitchen at the big house drinking out of highball glasses. It might have been five o'clock somewhere, but it was usually two o'clock here.

Mrs. McShane reserved her displays of affection for her doughy Skye Terrier, Digby. They owned a Basenji as well, one of those short-haired barkless African hounds they'd named Lamont. He moved around the place like a ghost, silent and dignified. He sniffed Nova just once and then retired to the side porch where he passed most of his time upon a weathered rattan couch.

Since Mrs. McShane's friends were all back in Dallas along with her hair dresser and her spin class teacher and the boutiques and the luncheon spots she liked, she and Michael hardly ever stayed for more than a few days. Except, of course, for their two-week visit in August when Mrs. McShane reliably flew back to Texas for the middle weekend, like a diver surfacing for air.

They didn't know anybody in Virginia except the people who worked for them and the cow man from out in the valley who pastured his herd on the estate. So whenever they had a dinner party, we were usually the guests, which Michael enjoyed but Mrs. McShane resented. Those were awkward evenings as a rule until the house painter got drunk. He was a Latvian who sang when he was loaded.

The chef's food was always overcooked and mediocre, a vodka-related problem I had to guess. Agatha and I sat next to each other. That was the pact we had. Michael was often on her other elbow. He seemed to appreciate on some level how spiritual and exotic she was while the chef and the wife just thought of her as the maid. Billy, for his part, passed those evenings feeding baguette to the dogs.

The McShanes had grown children who swooped in every now and again. A son and a daughter, both in their twenties, and mostly they just slept, though they each set aside a little time for making general havoc. The son tended to break fixtures -- light switches, and faucets, and towel racks. The daughter had short-term memory loss when it came to running tubs. She'd turn on the water and then get absorbed in a magazine or a TV show.

So I haunted the place when the kids were there, but it was usually just Michael, his wife, and their chef, Digby and Lamont. I'd pick them up at the Charlottesville airport in one of their Range Rovers and carry them back out there once they'd had enough.

When I'd come back in the empty car, then things would revert to normal. Agatha would have put the house in order by the time I'd returned, and we'd sit at the kitchen island, drink our coffee, and say nothing.

We had snow into early April, and I stayed busy plowing the driveway, clearing the porches, shoveling all the walks. The owners weren't due for a while, but that was my job, and I was conscientious about it, just like Agatha with her housework and Ben and Billy with their flowers. It was almost like we were working together to tend an elaborate grave. I went to the grocery store and the post office twice a week. I visited the Crozet library in a regular sort of way, and I hauled wood at winter prices as the pleading calls came in.

Me and Nova didn't see anybody beyond Agatha and Ben and Billy, so she didn't have much of a chance to attract strangers with her smile. It hardly broke her of the habit. I found her one morning romancing the meter reader who'd climbed out of his truck to sit in the driveway and play. But chiefly it was me and her, day after day and week after week, so we knew each other awfully well by the outright coming of spring.
Nova was looking filled out and proper sized by May. She'd grown into proportion, and her coat was thick and bright. On a proper collie, they would have called her color sable. She was a spirited girl who could run for miles if I'd give her leave to do it. By the coming of our first warm spell, we were both a little antsy for some real time in the woods.

I even had my Chevy running reliably by then. It would blow the occasional fuse, but otherwise it cranked and started, and it didn't leave me stranded on the road. I'd hauled a couple of dozen cords of wood throughout the winter, and I'd only ended up getting towed to the garage in Crozet once. So everything was right with my world, and once we had a warmish week, I loaded Nova in the Chevy and off we went for a spot of camping. I'd reached an age where I could sleep on the ground for one whole night in a row.

Carl had never cared for camping. I'd taken him on a trip or two, but he always loitered on the trail and complained about my pace. He had a rabbit he liked to bark at back home and a fluffy shearling bed. He didn't care for gritty water dipped out of a woodland spring and couldn't begin to see the point of passing an entire afternoon just walking.

Nova, by contrast, was eager for a hike, so I knew my primary challenge would be keeping her in sight.

We drove up the Jarman Gap Road and parked in a clearing at the top, continued on foot along the orange

blazed horse trail that took us past a gate post and into
the Shenandoah National Park. The ground was clear of
scrub, and the trees wouldn't be leafed out until the end
of June. It was cooler than I'd anticipated when we'd left
our house in the bottom, but once we'd hit the
Appalachian Trail and taken it north towards Turk's
Mountain, I managed a pace that heated me up
straightaway.

We pitched camp down off a fire road on the east
face of the mountain. The way I'd read my map, we'd
pass through Jerusalem Gap the following day. I set up
the tent and built a fire. I'd brought our dinner in foil
packets. Hamburger and onions and potatoes for me.
Leftover spaghetti for her. I cooked mine in the coals
and heated hers beside it. As we were eating, a bear
came wandering up, a cub as black as a mink. He was
about Nova's size. He was so busy pawing over rocks --
looking for grubs and bugs and such for dinner -- he
didn't know we were in the vicinity until Nova uncorked
a bark.

He did what bears do. I'd seen it countless times
before in the woods. He raised his head and looked at us
for about a quarter minute and seemed to go through an
ursine progress of "Oh. Right. Okay." Then he swung
around and bolted like he'd heard a starter's pistol and
the finish line was anywhere we weren't.

I had a grip on Nova's tail by then. She clearly
wanted to chase him, but I held tight, even once she'd
swung around and nipped my knuckles. Just a little
chewing with her front teeth in that collie sort of way.
She barked again. She quivered all over. That cub was
out of sight by then.

"We don't chase bears," I told her. "They just might
chase us back."

I slept like I usually do in the woods -- an hour at a
time. An owl woke me up. Then an opossum or
raccoon pawing around just outside. The deer were
snorting like dragons, and I kept hearing some kind of
nightjar. It was well off and away and sounded like a
woman in distress. I guess it was a wonder I slept at all.

Nova never woke up. She lay on her back and snored like a planing saw.

I'd intended to make pancakes for breakfast. They always seem like such a good idea when I'm packing for an outing, but then after a night in the woods I just want to climb in the truck and go home. It's all I can do to roll the tent up so it'll fit in the tote sack. I was achy and sore. A grown man isn't meant to sleep on an inch of foam, and it didn't help that my dog had shoved me around the tent floor through the night. What I wanted was a sausage biscuit and a cup of coffee from Homer's.

But for the fact the fire road was the shortest way to the truck, I probably would have put off Jerusalem Gap until my lumbar recovered. As it was, we had to walk right through it to get back where we'd started.

The Moorman River was high from snowmelt and early spring rain. The rest of the year, it was just a creek with a swimming hole or two. Nova waded more than I cared to. I crossed halfway on boulders and then shimmied on a fallen sycamore trunk. I rolled off a little sooner than I should have and sunk in an eddy up to my shins. I was still irritated about it halfway up the slope, and I threw down my pack and perched on it so I could wring my socks out.

It was midmorning by then, and the sun was just finding us. The mist was lifting towards the ridge line, and a couple of crows were raising a fuss. I had removed both of my boots and was peeling off my socks, when Nova and I together heard the shriek of a catamount. It was up in the rocks somewhere above the river and just wanted to let the two of us know it didn't approve of us much.

Nova failed to bark. She just rolled her eyes at me. For my part, I scanned the rockslide where I figured that cat would be, back in a crevasse probably and well hidden. Then below it I saw the sort of thing that snares your gaze in the forest, a patch of ground more orderly than the good Lord would have left it. Flat gray rocks on end in what looked, more or less, like rows.

"Oh," I said to Nova. "Jerusalem Gap."

I ended up counting eighty-six graves, certainly the biggest woodland cemetery I'd ever seen. It was too large to have been a family plot and too remote to have been a churchyard. I had to guess they'd plowed the fire road through it without knowing where they were.

It wasn't sad or unsettling to be there. The morning sunshine helped appreciably and the jolly tumble of the river surging below us. Laurels and rhododendrons were thick on the western slopes. There were wild azaleas in a sheltered depression off to the east. The trees about were chiefly massive, ancient white oaks, a whole grove of them whose canopies would join come June and shade the place.

I've never been a religious man, but that gap was speaking to me, was saying mostly, "You can get to heaven from here."

It was just another stretch of woodland for Nova. She treed a squirrel and chased two deer. She charged out of sight and left me with my thoughts and about four score of corpses that had come to be there for reasons I couldn't begin to figure out.

I shouldered my pack and made my slow way up along the fire road. After thirty yards, the place looked like just regular forest again. Nova was waiting for me along the spine of the ridge. She was sitting there smiling with her tongue dangling out the side of her mouth. We covered the mile or so back to the truck with both of us on the trail. Nova stretched out on the bench seat and slept all the way down to Homer's. The smell of my sausage biscuit finally woke her up.

We didn't trouble ourselves to camp after that but just went about our regular business. We'd take the truck out in the mornings, cross the pasture and stop at the forest edge. We'd hike in a little ways to pass a couple of hours cutting lap wood to length.

A few years ago, the McShanes sold off a good eighty acres of timber. The crew hauled out all the trunks and left the rest of it behind, even limbs as big around again as I was. Oak mostly, but some locust too and a little bit of hickory. I never had to cut a standing tree but just those limbs and leavings. It was my way of helping to clean the forest up.

I kept my splitter behind the barn, and I'd stack the wood back there. The McShanes burned all they wanted and let me sell the rest. I could usually move ten or twelve cords from mid November through March. More if I cared to, but cutting and splitting and hauling wood wore me out.

When the weather warmed, Ben and Billy would help with the flowerbeds. Me and Agatha were in charge of planting the garden. It was always cucumbers, banana peppers, and cherry tomato vines. We'd feed and water the plants by hand and spray them to keep the aphids away. The point was to have some produce handy for Mrs. McShane to pick in between breakfast and five o'clock somewhere.

This particular year, we had a full week of false spring which led Agatha, an island girl, to think it was time for us to fix the garden. By "us" she meant me and by "fix" she meant fight with the hateful tiller in the shed. That contraption made my Chevy seem like a Lamborghini. The tiller was all bad spark and weak combustion and sludge. To make matters worse it had a pull cord that wasn't even attached, one of those old-style ropes you wrapped yourself that came free when you yanked.

I'd usually have to take the engine apart and clean it to get the thing started, but I was fool enough each spring to think I could get away with less. So I passed my customary afternoon yanking on that cord, fiddling with the choke, cleaning the plug, raising blisters on my palms. I got irritated in my usual fashion and stalked away from the shed. I said hard things about that tiller as I climbed into my truck and drove out across the pasture to the tree line. I knew cutting wood would calm me, or leave me too tired to be mad.

Nova had a sensible fear of chainsaws and kept well away from mine. She'd usually wander off while I was cutting wood. Chase a deer. Tree a squirrel. Roll around in whatever stink she discovered. I'd pause to look for her every now and again. She'd be up along the hillside moving on a mission or just sprawled in the leaf litter waiting for me to get the sawing done.

This day I was exorcising my McShanes of Dallas upset. Who in the world had both hedge fund loot and a tiller with a pull cord? They'd been quick to put a restaurant range in the kitchen for their traveling chef, but they couldn't be bothered to buy proper twenty-first century equipment for the man planting all the vegetables their chef would overcook.

I was indignant in my way. I get indignant more than I ought to. In the end, I always realize I'm a dope. As I was standing there sawing a red oak limb, the indignation broke, and I confessed to myself that I'd never suggested that Michael buy a new tiller. I'd just stewed about the balky thing and had failed to complain aloud. So there I was irritated nobody had up and read my mind. Hardly the sort of thing worth getting overworked about.

That's just about when I resigned myself to taking the tiller apart, in keeping with my annual getting-the-garden-ready ordeal. I shut off my saw and set it down, threw a few sticks of wood in the truck. I heard Nova's deer bark from up on the hillside. She was yapping and bouncing on her front legs, and a buck was looking at her from across forty yards or so of broken ground. There were tree limbs between them, the scattered upper canopy of a locust that had been sawn away and left when the logging got done.

Bucks especially like to retire with a little dignity. They'll never just pivot and run unless a pack of dogs is on them. This one wanted Nova to know whatever direction he selected was where he would have been going anyway. A lone dog, he wanted her to understand, couldn't make him do a thing. Then he swung around and made a leap, shot up towards the ridge, and Nova went after him headlong, barking like wild.

She picked her way through the locust limbs and tried to jump over the last one. As I watched her gather herself, I was already saying, "No!"

A stout limb angled up caught her under the foreleg. It passed cleanly between two ribs and speared her. She hung on it for a moment until it snapped from her weight and she dropped to the ground. She landed on her feet and stood there. She never made a sound.

I was already moving at a run by then. The wood chips were flying off me, and I was stumbling up slope over rocks and slipping on the leaves. She walked a little my way, moving like her feet were sore. I half expected her to collapse and die before I had the chance to reach her. Of course, I was already blaming myself, blaming that tiller a little too. Why couldn't I have just stayed at the shed and disassembled the thing? Why couldn't it be the sort of tiller that would just up and start? I probably would have blamed Agatha a little if I'd abandoned sense entirely. It wasn't legitimate spring after all. The garden wasn't ready to be fixed.

Nova was standing when I reached her, and she looked embarrassed chiefly. I laid a hand on her, and she licked me. I expected blood, but there was hardly any at all. There was kind of a hole where the stick had gone in, just behind her front right leg. It had run at an angle along the length of her body, and there was a knot beside her left rear hip where it was poking her skin from inside. I could feel it. It might have just passed on through but for the plug of hair it was pushing. I couldn't help but imagine it skewering her liver, her kidneys, everything.

I was angry at myself. I was scared for her. I was heartsick and fearful I'd lose her. I resented the trash who'd put her out so she'd just end up like this. I didn't want to pick her up, but I doubted she could walk. So I did what I always do with animals and occasionally with humans. I talked to her. I told her the unvarnished truth.

"You're in some trouble," I said. "Help me know what you want to do."

I ended up following her down the slope. She walked like a creature who had no business in the woods. Slow and halting, picking her way, moving as if her pads were raw. She waited at the truck door and made me pick her up, did me the favor of keeping herself from crying out when I did. She stood on the truck seat as I eased out of the woods, crossed the pasture, and pulled into the driveway. I saw Agatha watching from the veranda as I gained the asphalt and gunned the truck.

V

Stuart's Draft seems close by until you need to get there quick. It's farther out in the valley than it has any need to be. I drove and drove, racing about as fast as my pickup could manage. I passed cars in places I wouldn't have ever thought of passing before. By the time I got near the clinic, I had a county policeman behind me. He'd started with the lights but had the siren going by the time I pulled into Walter's lot.

Nova had taken the whole ride standing, and but for the way she held herself, she still looked steady and reasonably all right. I lifted her out of the cab and set her down. She made her sore-footed way towards the clinic door. She knew where she needed to go as well as I did.

That cop stood up out of his cruiser and told me, "Sir," a couple of times.

I held up a finger to let him know I'd be back in a minute, and I was lucky he wasn't just a knucklehead with a badge. He nodded and stayed where he was. He said to me, "All right."

Even the receptionist with the complicated pile of hair knew this was no time for appointments. She went and got Walter herself, and they walked Nova into a treatment room. I told him everything I'd seen, showed him where the stick had gone in and where it had tried to come out. Walter nodded. He felt around. He walked her back for an x-ray.

That seemed to me as good a time to get arrested as not. So I stepped outside and joined Officer Crocker (it turned out) at his cruiser. I handed him my license before he'd bothered to ask for it.

"Problem?" he said.

I nodded and gave him an account of my afternoon.

He reached in his car and came out with a snapshot off the visor. It was a picture of a German Shepherd sitting on the bank of a pond. There wasn't anything distinguished about that photo. It wasn't even a good exposure, but it looked like it had been handled half to death.

"Brisco," Officer Crocker told me. "Lost him a year ago last month."

He handed me my license back. "Go on back in," he told me. "Walter'll do you right."

I was grateful to him, but I wasn't sure even Walter could mend her. When I stepped inside the woman with the regular hair escorted me into the back. Nova was stretched out in the surgery room, laying on a metal table. If I didn't know any better -- and I didn't -- I would have guessed she was dead.

"Put her under," Walter told me. He was looking at x-ray film. "Come here," he said, and I joined him at the light box on the wall.

The thing about a stick is that it doesn't really show up on an x-ray. It's not dense like teeth or bone and doesn't have the mass of an organ, so Nova's stick was just a vague and ghostly thing where nothing should have been.

"Might have nicked her liver," Walter told me. "I'm hoping it missed most everything else. Won't know until I open her up and see."

I was thinking I'd wait around, but Walter said he'd call me. Even once I'd left the building, I sat in the parking lot for a while.

"God," I said, "I hope she doesn't die." It wasn't a prayer exactly, just as near as I could manage.

I didn't know what to do but go back home. That's the direction I set out in anyway. I got as far as Waynesboro and stopped at the shopping plaza. Two years ago, it was a dairy farm. Then it got bought and bulldozed. Now it's all massive chain stores with too few people about to fill them up.

I went in the department store, and employees followed me through the place. At first I thought they were desperate to help me, but then I saw myself in a mirror. I was filthy and disheveled, with chain oil on my hands that I'd managed to rub on my face. I was on my way out, passing through women's delicates when my phone rang. I looked and saw that it was Walter calling.

There seemed a fair chance I wouldn't want to hear what I was about to be told. I stopped beside a woman who was sifting through bras big enough to haul gourds in. She didn't look remotely pleased to have the company.

"Hello." Walter was talking to somebody else. I could hear him. He was giving directions to one of the techs who worked in the back of the clinic.

"Walter," I said, but he went on talking. "Hey, Walter!"

"Oh," he told me finally. "Donald. Hi. Lucky girl. She's going to be all right."

"Dog's okay," I said to the woman beside me shopping for bras.

Most places you'd probably get yelled at or have security called on you. For all of its faults and failings, and this part of the world has many, a perfect stranger shopping for underclothes could still see fit to tell me, "Good."

Walter told me up front that he'd saved me the stick. It was just around nine inches long, and it had caused a lot less damage in the end than he had feared.

"It did hit her liver," he told me, "but just scratched it up a little. It went right under and in between everything else. Somebody's looking out for her."

"Guess so," I said.

"I'm meaning, of course, somebody other than you."

He wanted to keep her in the clinic and pump her full of antibiotics. He thought five days would do it, and I should visit her when I could.

"She won't like her cage," Walter told me. "You can walk her out back."

I felt like a different creature by the time I'd reached the lot. I drove east towards Afton and got off the highway at the top of the mountain. Though I'd never been over to Agatha's second job before, I felt certain I'd driven past her nursing home back when it was part of a business park that never caught on. I don't know why anyone thought Afton could use a business park. They couldn't even keep their IHop open.

So that nursing home had started out as some sort of office warren. Then it sat vacant for a year or two before it became a motor hotel. It was far enough from the Blue Ridge Parkway to be too much trouble to reach, so the motel failed and the building changed hands. It got renovated and refitted and turned into a nursing home, a golden-age storage facility called, cruelly, Evergreen.

They had nurses on staff and doctors on call, but mostly they had people like Agatha. The work needed kindness and patience more than authentic medical skill.

Evergreen sure wasn't easy to locate. You had to drive down the parkway a mile and then turn off to the left and swing back towards the entrance to the national park. Then you veered down a gravel track for maybe three or four hundred yards to a parcel of mountain that had been cleared and bulldozed and developed.

If grandma had to be packed away, there were worse places for her to end up. The view was little short of extraordinary. I parked and got out of the truck and wandered over to where the property sloped away. I was looking east and a little south, and once I got my bearings, I could see Charlottesville off and away to the left and beside it a hump of ground with a skinned spot on top that I knew for Monticello. Closer by, I could see estate houses that had been standing in Jefferson's day. Chiswell and Tiverton. Seven Oaks and Mirador.

If you ignored the interstate and the massive chicken farm down towards Lodebar, the countryside probably looked like it had two hundred years ago. Spring was coming, and the redbuds had bloomed already across the lowlands. It was nice just to stand there and take it all in after the near-death day I'd had.

The facility itself was low and laid out in wings. It was more welcoming than I'd expected a former motor hotel to be. The lawn was massive and planted with shrubs and flowers. There were colorfully painted Adirondack chairs scattered here and there out in the sun, and I could see residents sitting and wandering.

They were wrapped up in topcoats and winter hats against what felt like sixty-five degrees.

I spied Agatha well across the lawn steering a lady by her elbow. When I was nearly halfway to her, a man in a raincoat called me over. He was stuck in a sunflower yellow chair and lacked the strength to haul himself out. I stepped over to help him up. He had a walker with tennis balls on the feet and a purse on a shoestring around his neck. He told me he wanted a meatloaf plate with green beans and potatoes from the Basic City Diner and a couple of cartons of Salems because he was down to his last pack.

With that he opened his purse and dug out a buck and a half in quarters.

"Here," he said and dropped the coins in my palm. Then he sat back down. He didn't bend much but just tilted and dropped into his chair. I was afraid the thing might splinter underneath him, but he didn't seem concerned.

He dredged some phlegm and added, "Get yourself a little something."

I opened his purse and put the coins back in, made a vague apology. He told me I was a jackass, said it like a man who'd been calling people jackasses for years.

Agatha had seen me by then. Everybody out on the lawn had seen me by then. I appeared to be having a spirited effect upon them. They were like a flock of guineas, all cackle and alarm. I guess people rarely showed up and wandered across the Evergreen grounds. Everybody wanted to tell me something, most particularly the unhinged ones who were eager to hear if I had come to carry them out of that place for good.

I finally reached Agatha and gave her the blow-by-blow. I didn't let on to be any braver than I'd actually been.

Agatha patted me on the shoulder. Her bracelets jangled in a jolly and reassuring sort of way.

"Oh, Mr. Prickly," Agatha told me and hugged me close. She smelled like a spring bouquet.

I dressed for the visit the first time. I saddle soaped my brogans, and I wore a laundered shirt. I talked to Walter twice to try to get him to tell me when to come. I didn't want to keep Nova from eating or interrupt her rest, but Walter just told me, "I don't know. Whenever you want'll be good."

A part of my brain feared Nova might blame me a little. Carl had been perfectly happy to blame me for all sorts of things, from dinner being late to the trail being steep to the pain in his arthritic hips, and I didn't want to see in Nova's eyes Carl's variety of resentment. I certainly felt responsible, and I knew collies were awfully smart. If they could do geometry, why not recrimination?

So I was nervous and edgy, and I wanted her to be delirious to see me, even with a fresh surgical incision and an antibiotic IV drip. I knew it was a lot to ask of a dog, and I guess that's what was making me antsy. I know I took the long, slow route over the mountain to Stuart's Draft, and then I dawdled in the clinic lot and listened to the news.

I'd learned from Carl -- or gotten reminded by Carl anyway -- that it's never too early for me, in a relationship with a dog, to get myself ready for the day I'll lose him. I'd had a dog or two as a boy. One of them got hit by a car, and when the other grew old and halt, my father took him to a farm (he told us) where Rusty would sprawl in the sun and be just fine. My sister tried to explain to me why I was a fool to believe him, but a fool at that moment was the easier thing to be.

Carl, of course, let me off the hook by dying in his sleep. He'd been failing in his last half year but not in any dramatic ways. He'd grown creaky and thin, would spend all day by the wood stove if I let him, and he could barely muster the energy to antagonize the cat. I was sorry to lose him. We all were. We missed his brand of commentary and the fact that Carl had been more of a fur-bearing curmudgeon than a dog. The bond might have been fresher with Nova, but it was far stouter as well.

The receptionist with her hair piled up hadn't been expecting me. Walter had bypassed her like usual, and she looked a little surprised to find me shaved and smelling of bath soap. I didn't have an animal with me, so this wasn't about the cat. When I saw her checking the schedule on her computer screen, I volunteered, "Came by for a visit."

She had a policy against that sort of thing. She was a woman of rules. That's what made her a good receptionist and just a middling human being. Me and Walter together didn't have a rule between us. Whatever suited the circumstance was what we did.

So when she started in with, "I don't see you on the . . ."

I just told her, "Call him."

Walter then led me out a side door to a little, low building that served as the clinic kennel. There were a couple of cats in the bins by the doorway, and a basset hound in a cage just below them. He rolled his eyes up at us but seemed to lack the strength to stand. Nova was off to herself against the back wall. Her cage was raised on a shelf and eye level. I guess maybe I was hoping for a yelp when she saw me, but she just stood there and smiled.

Walter opened her door, reached in and disconnected her from her drip. I let him lift her out and set her down. He laid her on the cement floor to give me a look at her incision. It was a stem to sterner and ran from her chest nearly to her privates. Walter had made a neat job of sewing it shut, and it didn't look angry and red, but it was hard for me to see it. Hillbilly trash may have set her out on the roadside, but I was the one who'd let her get laid open from end to end.

Walter drew from his trouser pocket a length of stick. It was black where the blood had dried on it. He had the plug of hair it had pushed as well. Once I had them in hand, I could hardly conceive of how she'd managed to live.

Nova had no interest in the stick, could barely be troubled to sniff it. Instead she licked my hand. Not her rapid businesslike hey-Dad-you're-salty lick, but her slow affectionate lingering lick. She dragged her tongue across my knuckles with her eyes rolled up to watch me in a way I took to mean, "I feel you, Dad."

Walter led us out into the small back pasture where they kept all their oversized patients and various barnyard refugees. It was a weird assortment, and I'd been meaning to quiz Walter about it. Two donkeys. A trio of alpacas. A shaggy highland cow the color of an Irish Setter with a set of horns that spanned about five feet. Two Jersey calves. A camel. A quarter horse. A zebra.

"Up here somewhere's all right," Walter told us as he pointed towards a flat spot where the grass wasn't fouled with manure.

"Where'd that zebra come from?"

"Timberville."

"What was it doing over there?"

"Starving mostly. Somebody snatched it and brought it to us."

"And the camel and the shaggy cow?"

Walter shrugged. "Somewhere or another."

The camel chose at that moment to curl its lips and tell us, "Get the hell out." As rackets go, it sounded like a cross between a mule and pterodactyl.

"She's harmless," Walter assured me. "A little curious though."

I was going to press Walter to enlarge on camel curiosity, but the receptionist with the regular hair stuck her head out the clinic door to call him.

"A half an hour or so," he told me. "Just come get me, and I'll hook her back up."

Then he left me and Nova in the pasture with the menagerie, and she was too busy looking at all the creatures to even sit at first. I couldn't really blame her. That highland cow in particular had captured my attention. If he got next to you and turned around fast, you'd wish you were speared with a stick. I finally retired with Nova to the farthest corner of the pasture. I sat on a tuft of unmanured grass and induced her to lay alongside me.

She sniffed the air as I ruffled her coat. She looked over at me and smiled. I made a rather formal apology, and Nova toppled over at ease. She rolled onto her back and exposed her incision, which wounded me a little.

Slowly but relentlessly, the herd closed on us. The calves came over first, like skirmishers, just to see what we were up to. They crept in with their heads low, and once I'd told them both, "Hey, cow," they bucked and juked and pranced away as if I'd jabbed them with a prod.

Then the donkeys wandered over. The clean one hung back. The muddy one came straight up to sniff me. He just stood there breathing on me in his implacable donkey way. I told him I felt crowded, but I couldn't make him move. By then the alpacas had taken his flank and the massive highland cow was shaking the ground as he came up to join us. Then the horse came along. The camel and the zebra were the last to cross over. They all just stood and watched us while we sat and watched them back.

Nova had geometry to do with exotic variables to it, while I could just sit and study a camel and a shaggy cow up close. The zebra hung back a little, from me and from the animals too, as if he preferred to be suspicious of anything that wasn't striped.

It was a surreal few minutes. None of them bothered me for treats. They all just stood there and gawked impolitely at me and Nova together as if they'd wandered off the ark and we were the first things they had found.

I'd been around donkeys and calves and horses enough to know how to manage them, but I'll confess the rest of them made me uneasy. I didn't know if they were stompers or kickers or biters. I'd heard that camels spat and alpacas were always chewing people's ears. The highland cow had bangs and looked like a sullen teenager. I couldn't turn that into a good thing no matter how I tried. As for the zebra, I'd never expected to see one out of a zoo.

"Well, all right," I said and stood up from the ground. They all scattered but for the mules. A mule might run sometimes to food but never from anything. The muddy one and the clean one held their ground and waited for me to bring out carrots or apples or sugar cubes or something. I only had a stick of gum. I broke it in half and gave them each a piece.

Nova was moving well for a dog who'd had a nine inch stick pulled from her, and she followed me down to the gate and out to the landing by the clinic. I raised Walter, and he came out to help me put her in her cage. He plugged her antibiotic back in, and she drank water and stretched full out. I told her I'd be by tomorrow, and she let me leave without a fuss. She seemed to have enough sense to know that she was right where she needed to be.

I stopped at the big chain pet store in the shopping plaza. I must have browsed for half an hour before I found a dog toy I liked. It was a hard rubber knobby ball that didn't squeak, and I bought her a sack full of pig ears as well along with a blaze orange collar. Nova was chiefly brown and white, and she ran with deer all over. I don't know why I'd never worried before that she might be taken for one.

I'd forgotten my ex was due to come by for a cat visit. She was an every third Tuesday caller, and I came home to find her on my couch with Pom Pom in her lap.

"Where's . . . uh . . . ?"

I gave her a stunted version of all that had transpired because I knew she didn't actually give a hoot where the dog was or why. For her people, dogs had always been a category of livestock. Their setters might have been papered and pedigreed, but they never came in the house. She routinely held that out as the proper way to keep a canine. Why cats were spared that brand of family thinking I'll never know.

She let me tell her about my clinic visit, and instead of sympathy, she shook her head and said, "You and your dogs."

On one level, I liked to think the fact my ex came by each month was evidence we were both grown up and cordial. Maybe we hadn't been a lasting matrimonial fit, but we could still appreciate the finer qualities in each other and enjoy each other's company for one afternoon a month. But liking to think it and thinking it were two entirely different things.

She got around, like usual, to listing my failings for me. They came out like a catechism. I was stubborn. I was angry. I was unambitious. I was indifferent to her needs. I'd always been a poor provider. It was an exhaustive list, and I'd heard it once a month since we'd divorced. I'd lived it for six years ahead of that. She'd usually follow it up with her new husband Ronnie's virtues.

I'd run across Ronnie sometimes over in Waynesboro at the homewares store and occasionally at the Country Land Buffet. He'd shake his head and exhale hard every time he saw me. We were like a couple of journeyman boxers who'd both been in the ring with the champ.

Every morning at eleven a.m. for five days in a row, I drove to Stuart's Draft and sat with Nova in the small back pasture. The menagerie all got used to us, except maybe for the zebra. Of course, I'd decided that the zebra was the only one of them I wanted to touch. She remained standoffish throughout the week. She'd come over with everybody else, but she'd hang back while we were getting crowded by her colleagues.

The alpacas turned out to be a special plague in that regard. They'd come right up and step on you if you let them, and they smelled like a sweater you'd left in the laundry basket for a year. The camel turned out to be phlegmy in an unsavory sort of way, so I steered about as clear of him as I did of that shaggy highland cow. One of the calves grew bold and would lay down beside me at about arm's length, so I sort of found out how the cow man felt when he showed up on the estate and the herd came over to say hello and see what he had brought them.

Nova was better every day, a little more willing to roam the pasture and test her stamina. Walter had wrapped her up around her trunk with a stretchy sky-blue bandage, which the whole menagerie appeared to find enthralling. All of them, even the zebra, sniffed that bandage at least once. Nova would poke me with her nose when she had had enough, and I'd take her back into the low kennel building and put her in her cage.

Walter never told me exactly when I could carry Nova home. I just showed up one day -- I think it was the fifth visit I made -- and Walter came out to say, "She's good to go, I guess."

VI

She healed like a champ. I didn't have to keep her
from getting wet or over exerting. She seemed to know
what she needed to be about to make herself whole
again. Walter removed her topmost stitches after a
couple of weeks. All of the underlying ones melted, and
that scar stopped looking the least bit puffy after about a
month. Only then did Nova and I go back into the
woods.

I took her for the easy walk up to the ridge line and
the shortcut down the logging road back home. She
chased her first deer in a while. Though she wasn't
exactly tentative about it, she picked her way through the
scrub and the fallen limbs with more care than she might
have before. Even out in the open, along the trail, she
never went full tilt. She didn't appear to hurt anywhere.
Nova just seemed a little instructed and cautious as if a
stick through the ribs was precisely the thing to smarten
a collie up.

Unfortunately for me, she still saw fit to smile at
every stranger. She was a particular spectacle for a while
there with her elaborate sky-blue bandage, and whenever
we left the estate, I felt like I was squiring a starlet. I
worked up a little layman's patter on collie anatomy and
took to carrying the offending stick around on the
dashboard of the truck.

So the day the bandage went was a special day for
me. She kept on smiling, of course, and she could
always snag a stranger or three that way, but there were
plenty of people who'd glance at her and take her for
just a dog.

The Yancey Mills small engine guy rigged a starter
on the tiller. He took the engine apart and scoured it of
sludge, installed new gaskets and rings. He pronounced
it a fine old contraption, and it started for me like a
dream. So me and Agatha finally put in the garden, and

the boys got the flower beds in shape just before the McShanes and their dogs and their chef came winging in from Texas.

This trip, Michael decided he wanted a fieldstone grill in the backyard. Him and his wife had vacationed on a friend's ranch in Wyoming where Michael had suffered a fit of grill envy. He'd snapped photographs and had even sketched out plans. Michael felt sure we could build him a grill over the four days of his visit. In fact, all we did was gather rocks and level a piece of ground. It didn't help that Michael's daughter happened by to flood her bathroom.

So I ended up building Michael's fieldstone grill all alone. I resented it a little. I didn't believe my duties extended to building grills, and that's sort of how I ended up using Michael's mower at Agatha's nursing home. I managed to make myself believe I'd earned the right to do it. I just bent my thoughts around to what I needed them to be.

They'd had a lawn service up at Evergreen. It was two guys with a truck and a trailer who managed to run the thing off the mountain on a Friday afternoon. The evidence suggested they each had a couple of tall boys in them. They were coming down from Swannanoa, their last job of the week, and they ended up in a gully where the road took a sharp turn. Nobody got hurt, but the mowers and trimmers went down the mountain the hard way.

Everybody else in the area was booked up with mowing jobs, and when Agatha asked me if I knew anyone in the lawn care business, instead of just saying, "No," I offered to cut the grass myself.

I had to think Evergreen would eventually find somebody to take them on as a client. I was convinced I'd only have to mow up there once or twice. So I didn't hesitate to use Michael's fine lawn tractor. It'd only be for a couple of weeks, which seemed a fair trade for his grill.

So on a sunny Wednesday morning in the middle of June -- two weeks after the grass at Evergreen had last been cut -- I rolled Michael's mower up a couple of two

by eights into my truck bed, packed his string trimmer
and blower in alongside it, and headed up for Evergreen.
We'd had some warm June weather down in the bottom,
but it was coolish still up on the mountain, the sort of
weather fescue loves. Consequently, that big lawn was
thriving to the point of being overgrown, and the
patients were all out airing themselves in grass up to their
shinbones.

Nova planted her nose in my back and all but
shoved me out of the cab. She went tearing across the
parking lot towards about a dozen wobbly people, and I
wondered what would become of me if she knocked a
few of them down. Recriminations from their relatives.
Legal actions, I imagined. But Nova circled the group of
them twice around in her collie way and then selected a
woman taking her ease in a green Adirondack chair.
Nova slipped up beside her and gave her a lick and then
sat right down and smiled. I could hear that woman's
shriek of delight from over by the truck.

I'd been dwelling on the mowing alone and patting
myself on the back. Wouldn't I do a world of good?
Wasn't I the finest fellow? I hadn't gotten around to
thinking about what Nova might get up to. It only hit
me when that woman laughed like she'd spied a long lost
friend.

They must have had rules against dogs up there, but
nobody seemed to mind. Nova was prepared to lick and
smile at anybody who could stand it. She didn't care if
they were clear in their minds about who they were or
not.

That was what I would have known if I'd only
thought a little. Cutting the grass was all good and well.
Bringing Nova with me was the gift.

She was as happy at that moment as I would ever
see her. So many targets of dog opportunity, so many
slow-moving humans. She raced all around the lawn,
careful not to tip anyone over, and she smiled at
everybody, licked the ones who'd let her. She created the
jolliest uproar you'd ever want to hear.

Nova gave Agatha a gaudy hello. She did a twirl and
full dog caper and then treated the woman Agatha was

helping to a chair to a more subdued how-are-you and a supplemental lick. I don't think she neglected anybody. She circulated like collies will and lingered with those patients who appeared to wish she would. I was busy with the mower, trying to roll it from the truck and keep the thing from flipping over on me, so I left Nova to do whatever she might without me to supervise. I'd glance her way every now and again from over in the lot, but if she decided to chew on a geriatric, I was too far away to prevent it.

Fortunately for me, she was careful and kind. I was proud, of course, but relieved primarily. I couldn't take any credit for training her. She just happened to have impeccable manners and an admirable sense of decorum. I could see from the lot she was better with people than I could ever hope to be.

Agatha came over to greet me once she'd gotten her patient seated.

"I hope the dog's all right," I told her.

"She's lovely."

"No, I mean I hope it's okay that I brought her."

Agatha shrugged. "Mr. Borland," she told me, meaning the man who managed the place, "is in Richmond for the day. I don't think he'd care. Look at her."

We both watched her for a moment. She was having a sort of confab with a gentleman in a bathrobe. He had his hand on her head and was talking to her at some length. She sat and smiled up at him. She looked pleased to be petted and hear what he had to say.

We turned together towards the lawn to draw up a battle plan. We decided Agatha and her colleagues would shift everybody from the more lightly populated side of the yard. I'd mow it, and then they'd move the whole crowd off of the uncut half. It sounded easy enough, but the entire team was just Agatha and two colleagues. There was Denise who worked a little and slipped off to smoke a lot, and Matt from the high school in Waynesboro who went slack without instruction. He was content to stand and chew his fingers until somebody told him what to do.

There were leakage problems naturally and basic human complications. Most of the patients suddenly felt compelled to be where they'd been told not to go. Consequently, there were forays and feints, temporary escapes. I'd like to say I whistled and put Nova on patrol, had the wherewithal to direct her to gather up the strays and help Agatha and her colleagues hold the line. The truth is, I didn't do a thing but sit on Michael's mower. Nova did a world of gentle herding, but she did it on her own.

Agatha watched Nova licking and nudging and driving the patients a little, and she called out to congratulate me on the sterling work I'd done. The truth was Nova herded those patients because she was a creature born to herd. She did it with grace and affection because she was Nova.

Me and Agatha and Nova ended up doing just about everything ourselves. Matt was earning some sort of high school credit just for showing up. He'd decided anyway the showing up and the credit were related. Denise made a lot more noise about her general utility, but she was only marginally more useful than Matt.

Nova, consequently, got more of a workout than I would have suspected she might. She and Agatha had to keep the milling patients corralled, and it turned out they were pretty deft at milling. They didn't like being stuck in the gulag of their shaggy half of lawn. So I mowed as quickly as I could, polished off my half in twenty minutes, and the great migration began.

Agatha and Nova shifted everybody slowly to the freshly manicured half of the lawn. I mowed the other half. The whole job took an hour at the most, and that was including a little tidying up I did with the string trimmer. I had a blower as well, but the racket put some patients in a panic, so I just loaded it back on the truck with the tractor, the trimmer, and the planks.

I bought a soda from the vending machine in the lobby and just sat on the tailgate and watched. Agatha rarely stopped moving. She had an unerring sense of where she was required. A patient would turn to call out for her, and she'd already be halfway there. She laughed with them and listened to them. She reassured them as best she could, which was all in addition to seeing to their needs like a regular nurse. It was as if she'd thrown a party, and her guests were all infirm.

Nova went from patient to patient like a canine Agatha. She licked when that was needed, and otherwise she sat and smiled. She even came running to me to check and make sure I was okay, happy to be perched on the tailgate, satisfied with my soda. She poked my thigh with her nose and then went flying back to the lawn.

I couldn't help but notice there weren't any civilians around except for me. I didn't know if I was between visiting hours, but I surely didn't see any family. There was just staff and patients and me and my dog, and nobody otherwise. The vague melancholy over what we all come to in the end had just started taking hold when I heard from across the lawn an evil racket. Even if I'd never heard a rattlesnake before, I'd have known straightaway what it was.

The rattlers around here are gigantic. I don't know if it's the wealth of woodland vermin or the bracing mountain air, but our rattlers look like they migrated from the Amazon to plague us. They're routinely as big around as my forearm, and I've seen them three and a half feet long with a set of rattles the length of my ring finger. In the woods they'll usually just look at you, as if rattling is too much bother. I've nearly stepped on one or two just stretched out on the trail. But the ones you come across up in the yard or lurking in the shrubbery always coil and set up a Godawful fuss.

This one was trying to warn off a patient in a floral flannel housedress. She seemed oblivious to everything, including that massive snake. I couldn't see it from the truck, but it had to be near by her. Its rattle sounded like BBs shaken in a coffee can. Agatha certainly knew what it was. Maybe even Matt as well. It caused him to change the finger he was chewing. Denise was off in her corner having a Newport and a chat on her phone. Nova certainly knew there was trouble afoot.

I sprinted across the lawn and called to Nova as I went. I only caught a glimpse of that snake once Nova had crowded it a little and so had drawn it off the patient who'd strayed close in her housedress. Agatha eased in and pulled the woman away leaving just Nova to concern me. It would be a worry if she got bit, but rattlers rarely kill a dog. A dog might swell up and have some skin slough off, but if you pump them full of antihistamines they'll usually be all right.

It was a decent trade, but I was all for nobody getting bit, so I did a little hysterical yelling as I ran across the lawn. It was about the worst thing I could do since Nova looked at me and smiled when the sensible thing was to let that rattler monopolize her attention.

Like most timber rattlers, this one was pretty in its way. I don't know much about snakes, but I have to think it had recently shed its skin because its colors were almost cartoon bright -- all green and yellow and silver. I started telling myself what a pity it would be to kill the thing, but that was mostly because the only weapon I had was my multi tool. Also, I was well aware that snakes are territorial, and this one would get stepped on in due time. Likely by somebody too weak to recover from the bite.

"Have you got a hoe or a shovel or something?" I asked Agatha who told me they just had brooms.

I'd grabbed Nova by the collar, and we'd both stepped safely away by then, but the rattling was still going on in intermittent bursts. Nova was barking. Denise came stomping over to see the snake and let us all know what an inconvenience this sort of thing was for her. None of us saw the boy. He'd pulled up in his third-hand coupe. He'd climbed out and heard the snake. He'd brought his weapon off the floorboard.

He was just sixteen, as it turned out, and slight and bony. He looked the bookish, indoor sort. Then I saw his arm rocket, a slingshot with built-in forearm brace. Surgical tubing and a leather pocket he'd already loaded with a bearing. I could see the dull sheen of it in the afternoon sun.

He took concentrated aim from twenty feet away and let his bearing fly. The thunk of the thing was solid and satisfying against that serpent's skull. The rattling stopped precipitously because that snake was quite suddenly dead. If it could have had Xs on its eyes, it would have.

Here's what I liked about that boy: he seemed sad about it all. He didn't hoot or gloat. It was a heck of a shot, but he was sorry he'd had to make it.

"I hope that's all right," he told us.

Nova rushed over to assure him it was.

His name was Ethan, and he seemed downright embarrassed over the shot he'd made. Since he was uneasy talking to people, Ethan talked to Nova instead. She sat at his feet and smiled up at him while he told her about his neighbor's dog. A rattlesnake had bitten him once on the snout, and his whole head had swollen up.

"Like this," he said to Nova and described with his arms the circumference of a barrel. "He got all right mostly," he added, "but he'd been better before."

He wasn't rude and sullen like far too many kids I've strayed across. Ethan was just uneasy in his skin. Leery of people generally. Uncomfortable in conversation. I imagined he was happiest in his battered coupe with the radio turned all the way up.

"You're good with that slingshot," I told him.

He nodded and shrugged as if hitting a coiled snake in the head from twenty feet with a bearing was the sort of thing most anybody could do if he wanted.

"You must practice a lot."

"Yes sir."

"Who are you here to see?"

"My Gom," he told me and pointed to a woman, white-haired and tidy in her denim skirt, her cotton blouse and sweater. Agatha had made a point of introducing me to her already. She was Hattie Womble, a tidewater belle.

"You're Mrs. Womble's grandson?"

Ethan nodded. Together we watched Agatha walk with Ethan's grandmother out to her favorite chair beside a Rose of Sharon bush.

"Do you visit much?" I asked Ethan.

"Not on Tuesdays. I've got band."

I walked with him to where his Gom was sitting.

"He killed a snake for us," I said to Hattie Womble.
She laid a frail hand on my shirtsleeve and told me,
"That's nice."

VII

As the weeks passed, I got more interested in
Agatha's nursing home on Afton Mountain than I'd ever
imagined I could be. When I was honest with myself, I
knew it was largely due to Agatha. I was uncommonly
fond of her but was careful to keep from letting it on.
The longer I knew her, the more interesting she got, and
she had this carefree island way about her that was a fine
antidote to my constipated inland ways. Every now and
again she'd tell me about her daughter in Anguilla and
the man she'd once been married to who I only knew as
Brad.

Agatha had immigration problems that kept her
from visiting home. She tried to explain them to me
once, but I can barely figure out how to negotiate the
line at the DMV. I only knew she missed her daughter,
who visited Agatha once a year, and she seemed to have
flagging faith in Brad. She frequently hoped about him.
Hoped he'd meet his debts and obligations. Hoped he'd
feed their daughter well. Hoped he'd help her with her
schoolwork and keep her kind and decent. That hoping
was a last-ditch sort of thing but was all she could
manage from here.

Chiefly Agatha had me identify birds. The bright
ones reminded her of home, and in the spring we were
awash with goldfinches, tanagers, and blue birds. Just a
glimpse of one would delight her for a day.

The happiest I ever saw her was when I caught a
blue-tailed skink and shut it up in a pickle jar so she
could watch it be iridescent. It delighted her for an
entire day, and then she freed it in the boxwoods.

My ex didn't care for Agatha, which cemented my
affection for her. Agatha was exotic and conspicuously
pagan, and she was blessed with beautiful, unlined
caramel skin. That was the greatest offense to my ex
who fretted over her wrinkles. She was saving for

surgery to stretch herself smooth, but her handbag fetish kept getting in the way.

When I stopped back in to check on the grass up at the nursing home on Afton, I was certainly swinging by so I could say hello to Agatha, but there was something about that place, about the patients on the lawn, that functioned for me as an antidote to my solitary life on the estate. Nova got to go around and be ambassadorial while I was doing something authentically useful for civilians at large for a change. I feared that some of Nova's indiscriminate people love was rubbing off on me, but then I met Arthur Bigelow, and he helped to set me straight.

He remained a large man. Age and arthritis were trying to draw him down, but Arthur Bigelow refused to stoop and shrink. He still claimed to be six foot three. Five eleven was probably more like it. He had a shock of white hair that didn't appear to have seen a comb in years and enough wiry eyebrow growth for three or four people.

"Come here," was the first thing he ever said to me. He was sitting in a blue Adirondack chair and shaking his cane at the time.

Arthur didn't seem to care that I was well across the lawn talking to Mrs. Womble at that moment. She was busy confusing her grandson, Ethan, with his father, Dwight. Or rather, she was talking half about Ethan and half about his dad, blending them both together to make one person.

On her way to smoke a Newport, Denise bothered to butt in and tell Mrs. Womble, "You don't mean him, sugar."

Mrs. Womble was rubbing Nova's back and telling me about a collie named Sam her Dwight/Ethan had loved to pieces when Arthur Bigelow pivoted in his chair so he could look squarely at me. "I'm talking to you, mister," he said.

I went to him. What else could I do? He wanted to tell me how to mow. He informed me he'd watched me the other week and hadn't liked a thing I'd done.

"A man driving a tractor like you," he said, "hasn't ever been in the service."

I'd done a stint in the national guard, but it hardly seemed worth mentioning. Arthur Bigelow didn't appear to be hoping for a give and take. He had a few things on his mind, and all I needed was two ears.

Arthur preferred diagonal mowing, and he was pleased to tell me why. He liked to dress a lawn with chicken manure. "The stink don't bother me," he said.

He could tell by the ragged cut that my mower blades were dull, and he had to wonder what sort of life a man with dull mower blades was living. In Arthur Bigelow's view, I was probably leaving all my stones unturned, every little thing unsharpened and neglected.

"Thirty years in," he told me, most of them on a destroyer. He'd sunk submarines. He'd married a Formosan. He'd come back home to sell Oldsmobiles with his father's brother. Luther, his name was. Like me, apparently, Luther never did anything right.

Arthur Bigelow was the grumpiest man I'm sure I've ever met. If he'd ever had charm or courtesy, they'd fallen away through the years, and all that was left was unadorned bedrock. Whatever you were doing, you were doing it wrong. Whatever you believed, you were mistaken.

I don't quite know why I warmed to him, but I did at length and in time. There was little variety to his mood. Arthur was either more or less grumpy. But in what turned out to be eighty-six years of knocking around this earth, he'd done and seen a fairly wide variety of things. He was pleased to describe them given half a chance. Arthur Bigelow only needed me to sit for a bit and listen.

That was about all any of the patients at Evergreen truly wanted, particularly from an unattached civilian like myself. I wasn't family to anybody up there, wasn't paid to care for a soul. I was just on the grounds either cutting the grass or stopping in to watch it grow. I came with a dog who smiled and licked when it was called for. The Evergreen inmates were ready to embrace us. We only had to let them.

It turned out Arthur Bigelow had tended his share of lawns. He and his Formosan wife had moved around the area, and he'd grown rye and fescue in shaley soil, in red clay, in loose black upland loam.

Arthur provided me detailed instructions in conscientious mowing. He had opinions on top dressing and was agnostic about bagging clippings. "Did it when I had to," Arthur said. "Didn't have to much."

He had disapproved of the two boys who'd lost the job by wrecking their truck. "Always over there smoking with her." He sneered towards Denise as he said it. "Dumped their clippings in the woods." He pointed with his cane. "Rotted and stank something awful." Then he told me about a dish his wife used to make, some sort of Formosan hotpot. She'd died a while back. He couldn't remember when. "A day don't go by when I can't think of something or other I wished I'd told her."

That was the valuable thing about Arthur, the thing about all of them really. Even the hazy ones who could only remember themselves maybe half the time. They were all of them cautions against leaving anything on the table. It was a theme I'd hear over and over with only the particulars changed.

"What's Formosa like?" I asked Arthur.

He'd grown so accustomed to hitting moving targets with his talk that he seemed leery at first of easing into a description. He just wanted to answer me before I hurried away. I wrestled an Adirondack chair up alongside his own. "Never been there," I said as I sat down. "Don't know anything about it."

"December fourteenth. Nineteen and forty-four." With that, I was off with Arthur to the Pacific port of Keelung.

It was a lovely day to be sitting in the sun on a mountaintop. I'd forgotten about Nova. I located her alongside Mrs. Womble. Hattie was stroking Nova's head and talking to her. Telling her, I'm sure, about Ethan/Dwight and whatever else came to mind. She'd laugh whenever Nova gave her the slow lick on her wrist.

It got to where whenever I'd go up to mow the lawn at the retirement home, me and Nova would head out in the morning and spend the entire day. I made sure to take care of all my duties down on the estate. I worked longer and later the rest of the time to free up my Evergreen days. I painted the sun room, like Michael had asked me. I changed out all the faucet washers and recaulked all the tubs. I replaced the quarter round in the linen closet where the mice had gnawed it to splinters. I baited all the traps with fatback when the peanut butter stopped working. I patched the ceiling where the daughter had had her latest overflow.

I never would have guessed I'd so enjoy a day up on the mountain with the oldsters. Some of them were batty all the time. A few were lucid and nice/nasty. Women mostly who'd tell me sweetly, quoting Scripture even sometimes, exactly what sort of heathen fool and disappointment I was. I seemed to remind them of husbands or sons or the lowlives their daughters had married, and I was handy twice a month for whatever they cared to spew my way.

The men were of a vintage to have stints in the service to recount, but they were overwhelmingly outnumbered by the women. In addition to Arthur Bigelow, I only ever saw three other fellows. I know there were more inside in various states of dilapidation who didn't sit in the sun out on the lawn. Two of them passed away while I was still taking care of the grass. One in July and the other in early August. A hearse came rolling up both times from the funeral home in Waynesboro, and a pair of dandruffy fellows in cheap blue suits whisked the bodies away.

The patients never looked up. They must have made peace with the fact that they'd all take that ride in time.

Somehow that made the place less gloomy than it otherwise might have been. Patients up there didn't seem to fret about their health or prospects. They just made what they could of each passing day. I wasn't related to any of them and was meeting them all late in their lives. I didn't know who they'd been or how they'd lived, what they'd done with themselves before hand. I just knew what they told me they'd been about, and that was good enough for me.

A few of them had regular visitors, sons and daughters mostly. Ethan was the only grandchild I ever saw on the grounds who hadn't been made to come up and wasn't pouting the whole while. Ethan's father stopped by once while I was working on the lawn. He was Mrs. Womble's only son, and he and Ethan and Ethan's mother lived on the far side of Charlottesville, a little more than twenty miles away.

To hear Dwight tell it, he'd all but crossed an ocean to get to Afton, and Mrs. Womble couldn't be grateful enough to make him pleased he'd come. He stayed for nearly a half an hour and was on his phone most of the time.

That was the day Ethan gave me a slingshot lesson, the afternoon I first drew him out. He was a difficult child to talk to. It's hard to be sixteen, especially for a young man put together like Ethan. He was all knees and elbows and oversized feet. He was growing the sort of downy mustache my Great Aunt Bessie used to have, and he was pimply and oily and shaggy. Ethan had outgrown all his clothes. His shirttails wouldn't tuck in, and his trousers were too short.

On the inside, he was a little out of the ordinary for sixteen. He was not, that is to say, up to date in his interests and concerns. He knew his wildflowers. He was a birder with a passion for orienteering. He liked to wander in the deep woods with just a map and compass, park himself and see what happened by. He didn't play video games. He didn't read comic books. He had a head for math, a passion for bi-planes, and enough poetry in his soul to stand up on the lawn at Evergreen and take heed of the world around him.

The view south to the old estate houses down in the Rockfish Valley. The veins of basalt on the ridge line where the rockslides had kept the forest at bay. The red-tailed hawks that perched high in the trees overlooking the Evergreen lawn. And the inmates all around him -- not just his own grandmother -- but the whole slew of

them who Ethan treated like they just might have
something to say.

He wasn't a Yes Ma'm-No Ma'm sort of kid, polite
because he'd been instructed. He just happened to be
interested in people the way he was interested in birds.
But his voice was breaking and his skin was bad and he
was clumsy and gangly. You could look at a bird without
troubling yourself to engage in conversation. People had
this bothersome habit of always wanting to talk and
judge.

So I went at Ethan precisely where I knew he was
accomplished and asked him to teach me how to shoot
his slingshot half as well as he could.

He shrugged and mumbled there at first, glanced
darkly towards his father, but I prevailed upon him to
fetch his arm rocket out of his car. We went over across
the lot near Denise's ashtray corner. I pointed out a
poplar leaf on the lower limb of a far tree, a tree with
wooded hillside close behind it.

"Go on," I told Ethan. "Show me what you've
got."

He pulled a ball bearing from his pocket, pinched it
in the leather sling. He drew a bead on that poplar leaf
and paused to ask me, "Want a hole in it or need me to
knock it down."

"Knock it down," I told him, and that's what he did.
He hit the stem.

"How in the world did you learn to do that?"

Ethan shrugged. It was clear if I let him, shrugging
was all he'd ever do.

"Anybody teach you?"

He shook his head. "Picked it up in the back yard."

I pointed out another leaf. He put a hole in that one
for me.

"You hunt with it?"

"No sir. Nothing I want to kill."

Ethan glanced towards his father and his
grandmother. They were well across the lawn. His dad
still had his hand to his ear, talking on his cellphone.
Mrs. Womble was speaking to him. Me and Ethan

together saw her lay a hand to Dwight's forearm and saw
Dwight twitch and turn away.

"He's just busy, you know. Distracted," I said. I
wasn't sure why I felt the need to make excuses for
Ethan's dad. Maybe because I'd had a mother once, and
I'd been busy and distracted.

"Yeah," Ethan told me, which was his way of saying,
"You don't know the first thing about it."

"How are you aiming?" I asked him, getting back to
the slingshot, which was safer than family affairs.

He tried to show me, but Ethan was too eagle-eyed
for me. I'd reached an age where vanity kept me from
wearing the glasses I needed, so he'd point at something
for me to shoot, and I'd have to pretend I saw it. We
spent most of our time deciding if I was missing high or
left.

Denise showed up in her corner to smoke and asked
us why we were skulking around. When she didn't add a
"Sugar" or a "Honey" onto it to let us know she was just
joshing, I asked Ethan if he could load a bearing and
shoot the Newport out of her mouth.

"Doesn't really matter if you miss a little."

"I heard that!" Denise snapped and took a deep
toke.

By the time we reached the lawn, Ethan's father was
simultaneously conducting business on his phone and
saying goodbye to his mother. She attempted to put a
question to him when he showed her an upraised finger.

"Right," I heard him say, "with contingencies."

Once she'd seen Ethan approaching, Dwight all but
vanished for her. Ethan seemed to be the son she'd
always wanted and never had. I had to guess that's why
she stayed hard set to blend Dwight and Ethan together.
It was less confusion than wish fulfillment.

"Hey, Gom," Ethan told her and kissed her on the
cheek.

As Dwight finished his phone call, Ethan pointed at
me and said, "This is Mr. Atwell."

Ethan's father gave me a quick nod and that was it.
I was clearly not anybody he needed to know. He pecked
his mother on the cheek. "I'll get back when I can," he

told her and shook his head like it probably wouldn't be soon.

He didn't leave his mother occasion to tell him much of anything in return. "Home for supper?" he asked Ethan.

Ethan said, "I guess."

Then Dwight turned away and took a call. "Yeah," he said into his phone, and he was nattering on about some strain of legalese or another as he stalked off towards his car out in the lot.

It turned out Mrs. Womble had been some sort of local historical society bigwig. If Albemarle County has nothing else, it's got bucketfuls of history. People still come from around the world to visit Monticello and, truth be told, there are houses just as fine and of a similar vintage scattered in hollows and perched on hilltops all around the place. Ours was hardly the type of historical society any junior leaguer could run.

When I asked Mrs. Womble about the McShane's house, she told me, "She's a beautiful dog."

Nova was sitting at Mrs. Womble's feet, smiling up at the woman. Mrs. Womble was giving her a Hey, Sugar look and stroking the side of her head.

Ethan glanced at me and pointed at his ear. I'd decided Mrs. Womble was confused and a bit demented when it turned out she was chiefly hard of hearing. I asked her again with volume about the house that I took care of.

"Built by Fitzhughs," she told me. "1792."

The bronze plaque on the gatepost said 1810. I had to think if the previous owner, who had that plaque engraved, could have added eighteen years of pedigree, he surely would have.

"It burned," Mrs. Womble added before I'd asked about the date. "Rebuilt by Willoughbys in 1810. They'd had a few reversals. Went a little cheap."

Nova gave Mrs. Womble a slow, loving lick. "Aren't you the sweetest girl," she said.

I took leave of Mrs. Womble at such full volume that Arthur Bigelow shook his cane at me from well

across the lawn, waved me over to him so he could say,
"Pipe down!"

I was in the big house the day after Mrs. Womble
had told me about the Fitzhughs and the Willoughbys,
had gone in to check on the plumbing and gather the
dead mice. We had something in the crawlspace. I was
figuring a rat, and I'd set a cage trap for him. When I
crawled through the access door to check it, however, I
discovered I'd caught a weasel. At least I thought it was
a weasel. I'd never seen one in the wild.

I set the cage out on the redwood picnic table in the
side yard and left Nova outside to watch our creature
while I went into the house. Michael kept a full
compliment of field guides in the room he called his
study. It did have a bookcase and what passed for a
desk, but in truth it was all about the massive flat screen
television where Michael watched football and tennis,
closing stock prices and nothing else.

The Audubon Society helped me out with all the
weasel particulars I needed. Ours was a black-tipped
long-tailed weasel, the Mustela Frenata, and according to
the book the thing "occurred" about anywhere it
pleased. They lived for but a scant three years, mostly in
woodlands near water.

I was sticking that book back up on the shelf -- the
whole cabinet was original to the house -- when I
noticed the backing for it was rough-sawn timber mill
stock. That reminded me of what Mrs. Womble had said
about the Willoughby's reversal of fortune, and I spent
the ensuing hour wandering around the house locating
all the spots where the builders had gone "budget" by
early nineteenth century standards.

They'd been frugal at the timber mill and had
compensated with plaster. There was a Yankee floor in
the dining room, hidden by a rug. They'd used heart
pine on the outer bands, but where the table sat, it was
slab wood and mill trash planed a little and fitted in
however it might. The ceilings were maybe a foot lower
than in similar houses I'd seen, and the rooms were laid
out on a slightly smaller scale. The Willoughby's only
extravagance appeared to be their soaring front hall.

So I'd learned a thing up at Evergreen from, to my mind, an unlikely source, and I was anxious to tell somebody all about it. Since Agatha and Ben and Billy weren't due for another week, I ended up giving Nova and our new weasel friend a bit of a history lesson on our way across the pasture. Nova took it well enough, but the weasel went dead frantic. I guess he thought he was about to meet his end.

Instead, I carried him through the pasture to a creek on the far side. It had clammy locusts along its banks that would have to pass for woodland. I thought he'd be sheltered enough anyway to keep him safe from owls and hawks until he could get his bearings and burrow or nest or flee.

He was wheeling around so in the cage that I was reluctant to let him out. I made Nova retreat up the slope and sit at what looked a safe distance. Then I had a word with the weasel, but it didn't seem to calm him. He appeared to believe I was about to plunge him in the creek and drown him, and the only way I could change his mind was to raise the door and let him out. Even then, he clung to the cage, and I had to shake him free.

He sat on a tuft of pasture grass and looked at me for a moment as if I owed him an explanation for having carried him out of the house.

"Go on," I told him. "Do whatever it is you weasels do."

I was halfway up the hill before I noticed he was following me towards the barn. I set Nova on him, and she circled him round and herded him to the creek.

It didn't help in the end. He'd returned to the powder room wall not two days later. He didn't gnaw like a rat or make a lot of racket. He'd climb in at night and sleep there, go out in the morning on the prowl. I caught him once more in the trap but just let him back into the crawl space.

It seemed to me if I could deputize a black snake, I could deputize a weasel as well.

VIII

I'm just not a killer. I wasn't raised to hunt. My
father was a painting contractor and a weekend piano
player. He couldn't keep good help, by which I mean
anybody reliably sober, so he hired me at family rates
once I was old enough to work. I stayed with him for
eight summers straight, and we'd prep and paint all day
while saying next to nothing to each other. My father
preferred to work through chord progressions in his
head. His dream was to be a full-time musician.

"The next Teddy Wilson," he'd tell me.

By the time my father wanted to be the next one,
Teddy Wilson had retired and been forgotten. He'd
played most notably with Benny Goodman, but that was
decades back, and it wasn't anywhere near the
Shenandoah Valley where you could find bluegrass if you
looked hard enough but rarely big band or jazz.

The question my mother would put to my father -- a
little too often, in truth -- was "Let's say you're the next
Teddy Wilson. Then what?" It seemed clear to her the
next Teddy Wilson would end up painting houses.

"A man's got to have his passion," was all my father
would ever tell her, usually on his way to the basement to
noodle on his out-of-tune upright.

I saw him play in a club in Roanoke once. It was the
high point of his career. He'd put a trio together with a
couple of buddies. One of them wanted to be the next
Lester Young, the other the next Charles Mingus. They
came about as close as three white guys could to tearing
up the place.

My father had a heart attack or something down in
the basement one night. My mother thought he was
working up charts and didn't find him until the next
morning.

He taught me how to use a sash brush and play
passable boogie woogie, but he never took me hunting

when the season came around. I went with our neighbor once. He had a son about my age, and we lurked in the woods all day and came out late afternoon with a doe. The son, Neal, had shot it. He was a cruel dimwit, and it didn't seem right to let him aim a gun at anything.

His daddy rubbed deer blood on him, and we carried the carcass to the butcher. Then they went home to throw last year's freezer-burned venison away.

I couldn't see the point of it even back then when shooting a gun should have thrilled me. Now deer season serves as ongoing state-sanctioned cracker high holidays. In the past few years, I've run up on scores of trespassing drunken hunters. Most of them give me some variation on the prevailing local line: "My granddaddy used to hunt here." As if a century of title and deed conveyance had never happened at all.

The majority of local hunters these days can't even be troubled to get out of their trucks. They'll park on a logging road and wait on a deer to run past them through the trees. They'll shoot it out the window and cut it open, remove the saddle and tenderloins. They'll leave the carcass to rot where it fell. Since it's hard to see any sport in much of it, there's little I like better than snatching a rifle from one of those blaze orange fools I meet in Michael's woods. If he mouths off enough, I'll shove the barrel between forked limbs and bend it.

My message is always the same. "Your granddaddy's dead and gone."

They're usually too full of Wild Turkey to do anything but sputter back.

Only once was I ever obliged to do violence to hunter and rifle both. This one threatened Carl, assured me he'd return one day and shoot him. I made sure he'd have to do it with fewer teeth.

I don't mean to say I love deer. We're overrun with them. They eat all the apples and nectarines out of the old orchard in the spring and they strip the shrubbery bare throughout the winter. But they're just part of the world the good Lord made, and I've got a Harris Teeter, so I don't really need to shoot deer to get by.

While I might have had a rifle under my bed, I didn't fire it much. It was an old Enfield with a walnut stock, and the bullets were British and pricey. Every time I squeezed off a round my wallet hurt.

Then one of the cow man's Galloways went down, and I had to kill something after all.

We were all at the house. It was Thursday, and Ben and Billy had just reflowered the foyer. We were deep in July, and the boys had come around with summer's lavish bounty. I'd never seen snapdragons and gladiolas in the colors that they brought, and they had leafy foliage and gnarled architectural vines. They made a showpiece out on the banister cap that people would have found astounding if people had known any reason to drop by.

It was my day for lunch. I knew they expected food I'd bought and brought in. I'd only ever cooked lunch once before. I'd made a turkey meatloaf. It had looked delectable on the outside but proved desiccated under the crust. So dry, in fact, that even Carl wouldn't eat it. They all seemed to think it was settled that I would only buy lunch after that.

But I was ready for redemption. That meatloaf was a year and a half behind me, and I'd purchased some shrimp from a fellow who was selling it out of his truck. There's a pullout on the road that comes down off Afton Mountain, a wide gravel lot where semis stop to let their brakes cool off, and people set up folding tables freighted with junk they hope to sell. Every now and then a guy in a refrigerator truck with "Fresh Fish" painted on the side shows up there and stays a day or two. I'd seen people buy what he was selling, and they'd all looked normal enough.

I'd already been thinking about cooking lunch when I saw him and stopped in. He claimed to be from Ocracoke, but he had West Virginia tags and that shifty, back-hollow Allegheny way about him. He was selling flounder and blue crabs, shark steaks and scallops and three different sizes of shrimp. When he opened the back truck door, the smell didn't knock me over, so I bought a few a pounds of U-18s to carry back for lunch.

I peeled those shrimp. I cleaned and skewered them. I marinated them in a sauce that my lone cookbook called "Caribbean" because, as best I could figure, of the coconut flakes that I didn't have and couldn't add.

I could tell by the way Ben and Billy and Agatha looked at each other when I showed them my skewers that my dry turkey meatloaf was plaguing the three of them still.

"What's that?"

"Caribbean shrimp."

"What's in it?"

"Orange juice and rum," I told them. "Garlic and stuff."

Billy stuck a finger right down in the marinade. He sniffed it. He turned it in the light to study its unctuousness. He glanced at Ben and Agatha before putting his finger to his tongue in an irritating we-who-are-about-to-die-salute-you sort of way.

"Hmm," he said. "That's different."

"Where'd you get your shrimp?" Ben wanted to know.

"James River," I told him. "Caught them all in a sock."

"I'm just asking," he said and threw up his hands.

"You didn't get these from that guy in the truck, did you?" Billy asked.

"You want me to go buy some barbecue?" Like I said, I have indignation down.

With that I went out to light the grill, the new fieldstone grill my Caribbean shrimp would put to good use. I left the three of them in the kitchen to strategize if they wanted about what they would and wouldn't put in their mouths.

I'll admit I was a little steamed. I didn't think of myself as just the mousetrap, plumbing leaks, and mower guy. Maybe I couldn't cook as well as they all could, but I could cook a little.

"We'll just see," I said as I lit the gas and settled the hood back down. I thought I was talking to Nova, but it turned out she'd stayed in the house to conspire with the rest of them.

So I was peeved and wallowing a little when I first saw that cow. She was stretched out on the ground, resting on her belly. The rest of the herd was out of sight, beyond the barn I had to guess. Some of the cows had dropped calves into June, but that season was well over, and I remember watching that downed heifer for a bit and not liking the sight of her much.

But I had shrimp to cook and culinary slights to mull about, so I put her from my mind and focused on my skewers. I tested the shrimp by eating a few, and they tasted rummy to me. In truth, they tasted like a blend of alcohol and ammonia with faint coriander notes. They were not, that is to say, delicious, so I made it my job to guarantee that at least they wouldn't be dry.

I carried the skewers into the kitchen piled up on a platter, and I had just begun to unload my caveats and qualifications when Ben and Billy and Agatha cut me off in such a way as to let me know they were primed to make a show of enjoying whatever I'd brought them. Even shrimp that had passed through the hollows of West Virginia to get onto their plates.

I can't say we enjoyed the shrimp. Even I just pushed it around. It wasn't as bad as the turkey meatloaf, but it was deplorable enough. I was over at the counter scraping leftover shrimp into the garbage when I noticed that cow hadn't moved a jot and was splayed out in a funny sort of way.

"Know anything about cows?" I asked.

It was Ben who joined me at the sink. We watched her for a solid minute.

"Where's everybody else?" Ben asked.

I motioned to let him know the rest of the herd was up beyond the barn.

"Let's have a look."

So me and Ben and Nova went out to inspect that cow. I could tell by the way Nova behaved she knew something was out of kilter. She usually pricked up whenever she entered the pasture, but this time she eyed that downed cow and dispensed with all her math. She even hung back a little and let me and Ben lead the way. The cow, for her part, heard us coming and swung her head around and lowed.

I don't know awfully much about the anatomy of cows, but even I could tell by the way she sprawled that cow had gotten out of alignment. She tried to get up as we approached, so we stopped in a bid to calm her. Nova seemed to know that the best she could do at that moment was hang back. She sat down in the pasture and let us slip on up the hill without her.

We got within about ten feet, and that was the best we could do. That cow was mooing so that she was drawing the rest of the herd. No matter how frantic she got, she couldn't really seem to budge.

"Her back legs won't work," I said to Ben.

"What do we do?"

"Call the cow man."

We went back to the kitchen where I'd left my phone, and I put in a call to the cow man. I told him what we'd found and was beginning to describe that cow when the cow man told me, "Broke down. No help for it. Your dog didn't run her did it?"

"Not a chance," I told him.

Then he asked me, "How's the weather over there?" There wasn't a thing in this world that could keep the cow man from talking about the weather.

"Nice enough," I said, which he let serve as invitation to tell me about the sort of day he was enjoying down in Nelson County where, remarkably, the weather was identical to our own.

Once he'd left a gap, and it was a long time coming, I asked him, "You want me to do anything?"

"Yeah, I guess," he told me. "Go on and shoot her." He said it like he'd asked me to roll up his windows or gather his mail.

"Shoot her?"

"Nothing else to do. I can't get there before tomorrow."

"Maybe we ought to wait."

"Naw," he said. "No sense in making her suffer."

I couldn't argue with that. "Shoot her where exactly."

"Right in the head," he told me and then said to me, "Hold on." With that he began to talk to some fellow wherever he was at that moment. They were debating whether or not they had much hope between them of rain. They laughed about something, and then he came back to me. "You got a rifle, don't you?"

"Yeah. I guess I'll take care of it. I'll go on and bury her too."

"I appreciate you," the cow man told me. "Got some thunderheads coming up here." I punctuated the meteorological prattle by shutting my phone off.

"Shoot her?" Ben asked.

I nodded.

"Got a big enough gun?" Billy wanted to know.

"I hope so." What did I know from shooting cows?

I went and fetched my Enfield. Nova came along with me. The clip only held five bullets, but I guessed that would be enough.

"Come on," I told Nova with my rifle on my shoulder, and we walked together back to the big house where Agatha and Ben and Billy were waiting for us on the porch.

"Want me to go with you?" Ben asked me in a way that let me know he hoped I wouldn't.

"Mr. Prickly needs us," Agatha said, and she took Ben's hand and led him down the steps.

"You're fine there," I told Billy, who didn't have the stomach for such things.

"And over there?" he asked me, pointing to a far corner of the porch from where he was sure to have a view of nothing but the siding.

Agatha looped her free arm in mine, and the three of us passed through the pasture gate with Nova just behind. She sat down in the pasture like she had before and watched us go on ahead. This time that heifer didn't try to get up. She seemed to know what was coming.

She let Agatha stroke her. Even the cow man himself didn't really get to touch his herd. They'd gather around him but shy away whenever he reached out for them. If he wanted to lay a hand to a cow, he had to pen it up. Not Agatha. She stroked that girl and leaned close to tell it something.

"She's ready," Agatha told me before taking Ben's arm and backing with him well down the hill.

So it was just me and her. She was good enough not to look up at me. Instead she showed me the flat of her boney head. I held the barrel of the rifle mere inches from it. I closed my eyes and fired.

Most of the herd was watching me from over by the barn, but not with any special, fearful interest. They were cows, after all -- a beast created to make a horse look smart. They milled around a little and then wandered over towards the pond. I didn't look down until I felt sure that heifer was dead and still. Nova only came up then to do a little sniffing. I doubt she'd ever had the chance to nose a cow up close, and she availed herself of this one with considerable canine rigor.

Nobody said a word. That cow collapsed as all the life drained from it, deflated almost until it was just a pile of meat and fur.

Agatha came up to me and kissed me on the cheek. "Thank you, Mr. Prickly," she told me.

Ben had gotten more than he'd bargained for. He'd just come for flowers and lunch. He shook his head and worked his jaw. "Can't hear a thing," he said.

Billy ventured up now that the shooting was done. "That's a lot of meatloaf," he told me. "You get to keep it?"

I shook my head. "She's going in the ground."

I drove the backhoe out of the barn and dug as close to that cow as I dared. Then I rolled her over with the bucket and dropped her neatly in her hole. So neatly, in fact, that I wasn't obliged to lay on the bucket and pack her. That made it seem less like livestock disposal and more like a burial.

Agatha had me switch off the backhoe so she could say a little something. She led us all in a benediction, and then she invited Ben and Billy and me to throw in with whatever we wished. As a trio of practicing heathens, we didn't have much ammunition.

Billy finally spoke for the three of us. He said, "Bye, cow."

IX

I figured I had one more chance to borrow the mower before the McShanes showed up for their two weeks in August, so a few days after I'd put the cow down, Nova and I drove up the mountain to pay a call at Evergreen.

I knew everybody up there by then, so there was a little bit of lawn care and a whole lot of social call. I liked to get the mowing out of the way, and we had our system down where Matt and Agatha (Denise every now and again in between Newports) would shift the patients around as I cut the grass.

When it worked, and it often did work well, watching the choreography was like seeing a good nurse make a bed with a patient in it.

It was usually just forty minutes of mowing and two hours of everything else. That would include trimming and tidying up, but it would be chatting mostly. Some of the patients rarely saw anybody except for the regular staff and me, and they all had things to tell me, stuff they'd accumulated in between visits.

My job, as I saw it, was not just to listen but to live for a time in their world. Nova's job was to circulate and smile, to lick when licking was called for, and to respond to any dog name a patient happened to shout out.

Twice a month up at Evergreen I managed to feel a little like a doctor on rounds. A doctor who smelled of gasoline and freshly mown fescue, but I could listen to Mrs. Mathers tell me all about her kidneys which needed, in her view, a new wiring harness and maybe a thirty-amp fuse. I'd tell her I'd check her warranty and get back with her shortly. That was all she wanted to hear, and a degree from Johns Hopkins wouldn't have helped. Most patients just needed somebody to sit for a minute and hear them out.

I had favorites, of course, but I tried to spend a little time all over. I usually ended up with Mrs. Womble after Ethan had arrived. He came by every day but Tuesday. I always saw him when I mowed, and he'd sit for an hour or two on the lawn with his grandmother.

Nova held Mrs. Womble in special esteem as well. She must have had the sort of touch that spoke well of her to Nova. She liked to rest her hand on Nova's head, and she'd talk to her like I talked to her, as if she were somebody. No topic could occur to her that the dog didn't need to hear about. So usually I ended up talking to Ethan while his grandmother talked to the dog. She gave Nova an ongoing lesson in the history of the county while Ethan taught me that sixteen-year-olds weren't required by law to be a trial.

Ethan read books. Actual books. Not "graphic novels." He didn't live to play video games. There was a girl at school he liked. He was fueled by curiosity and was unfailingly polite. He loved his grandmother, and while he didn't seem to resent his father, he was more than a little skeptical of the way his parents lived.

I don't know why it took me so long. I'd been meaning to ask her for some weeks, but I finally got around to mentioning to Hattie Womble Jerusalem Gap. She was up on the local estates and the Virginia dignitaries. It seemed a reach to hope she'd know anything about graveyards in the woods.

"Ever hear of the place?" I wanted to know.

"Oh my, yes," she said. Then she smiled at the dog, scratched her ears, and broke into song.

It sounded to me like a highland lament. She couldn't remember all the words, so she sang out and just hummed by turns. It was a song about a beauty spot down in a glen, a sacred place where somebody fine and holy had died for something or another. He'd been buried where he fell, and his true love ended up getting laid beside him. It got to where people from all around ended up joining them there.

Beyond the lyrics, Mrs. Womble couldn't remember the particulars with much depth.

"I think it was over a young lady," she told me. "Isn't it always about a young lady?" She went on to describe in fuzzy outline a Montague/Capulet sort of thing.

It seems the upland Romeo got struck down, and though he was decent as far as it went, he wasn't abidingly memorable until his grave began to sprout.

"Coralroot orchids," Mrs. Womble said.

She told me they covered the ground where he lay.

"You can go a lifetime around here and never see one," she added.

Ethan, who was up on plants in a way a teenager rarely is, said he'd only ever seen a coralroot orchid in a book.

"And the ones in the gap are yellow," his grandmother informed him.

"No!" Ethan said, and she nodded to assure him it was true.

While I had come to be aware that even cat pee couldn't kill an aspidistra, that was about the only plant-related thing I knew for sure.

Mrs. Womble sang her song again, with fewer words this time while Ethan told me all about the yellow Wisters coralroot orchid which, unlike other coralroot orchids, didn't live on fungus alone. The rest of them had no leaves and no chlorophyl while the Wisters had a little of both. It was a kind of miraculous hybrid depending on sunlight and fungus together.

"A botanical miracle?" I asked Ethan. I suspected I knew the answer already. People had asked to get buried down in Jerusalem Gap not because of the boy who'd died -- for love or honor or something very much like them -- but more because the orchids he'd fertilized were yellow. And the yellow ones were doubly precious for being exceedingly rare.

Ethan wanted me to show him where this place was. I could actually see the western contour of it from where we were sitting. We had a view of a stretch of ridge line that reached into the park, and I pointed out a slope that lay slightly south of the park entrance.

"See that vein of rock?" I asked him. "It's about straight down from that."

Hattie was the one who made me point it out again. She asked me to calculate the distance and supply her with landmarks. Just the sort of things a local historical maven would want to know.

Since Ethan didn't think he could find it on his own, I promised to take him, and when I got home, I called Ben straightaway. Aside from the Montague/Capulet thing, I couldn't tell him much he didn't already know. Him and Billy never gathered coralroot orchids because they withered and died straightaway, but he was familiar with them and knew the spot in the gap where they grew. He'd just never heard the local story about how they'd wound up there.

Ben allowed he was ready for a trip to the gap to see what was still in bloom. I set it all up. I was pleased with myself because Ben and Billy seemed the sort of people who could persuade Ethan by example. They'd made a fine career of flowers and plants. They were proof you didn't have to be a lawyer. You didn't have to neglect your mother. You didn't have to live on your phone. And I'd get to visit the deep woods without having to sleep on my foam mattress with Nova shoving me around the tent all night and knobby rocks sticking through.

Ethan came out to the McShane's place and rode up with me and Nova in the truck. We met Ben and Billy at the wide spot where the Jarman's Gap Road ends, and they all hit it off like I'd figured Wister coralroot orchids fans would. Nova saw three deer immediately and tore out down the trail, raced full bore into the national park proper.

On my only other visit to Jerusalem Gap, I'd come from the opposite direction. So I let Ben take the lead with Ethan, and they talked wildflowers the whole way. Billy, for his part, was fixed on stepping exclusively upon the ground, as opposed to the scaly back of a woodland reptile. He was so focused on where he put his feet that he kept missing the limbs and the brambles, and I made it my job to keep Billy from plowing headfirst into stuff.

It had been dry for the last few weeks. Not even the cow man could bring rain, so the fire road wasn't as weedy and overgrown as it might have been. The woods generally were looking a little late-July tired. Under-irrigated and over-heated, wind beaten and marginally ragged, but the state of things transformed once we had plunged into the gap.

I'd done an awful lot of hiking in my day, but I was usually storming through. Trying to make my miles and get to the next campsite. I was speedy and efficient, and I thought I was observant, but the woods were the woods to me when I was thundering through them on foot. Just ground to cover and conquer, weekends to eat up. I thought forests looked more or less the same, and then we got to Jerusalem Gap. Once we'd come down off the ridge and into the hollow proper, I could see that the woods around me didn't look like the woods above.

It helped that Ben was showing us the changes in the flora. A plant that hadn't been blooming ten yards back was blooming ten yards farther on. The air felt different. Cooler. Damper. The fire road was suddenly choked with weeds. The canopy was fuller overhead than it had been before, and sunlight fell in miserly shafts and patches. Ben found the first orchid before we'd even reached the graveyard proper. It wasn't the yellow rare one but the ruby striped one instead which people ran across once in a blue moon instead of -- as with the yellow one -- hardly ever at all.

Ben and Ethan squatted to study the blossoms. Billy thought he heard a snake. Nova gave chase to something out of sight well down the fire road. We could hear it crashing through the brush before we finally saw it -- an adolescent bear she sent scrambling up an oak. A gust of wind swept through and stirred the leaves, and it wasn't the sort of furnace blast we'd been enduring down below. It was cool and damp and unexpected. Almost otherworldly.

Ben started gathering vines and ferns and all sorts of scattershot foliage. Most of it Ethan could call by name and did. Billy stayed too busy worrying about where to put his feet to even begin to harvest plants and place his hands in peril.

"You'll be all right," I told him. "Just walk where I walk."

So he got right behind me and put his feet precisely where mine had just been. That's how we continued down the road, and I almost missed the gravestones. They were lost in the underbrush, barely peeking through. They looked even more natural and accidental than when I'd seen them in the spring.

Together me and Ethan sang as much of his grandmother's song as we could remember, and it was Billy who found the yellow orchids sprouting in the scrub.

They were growing on a grave, more or less. They were flared out from a rock that looked a little like a headstone. There was a rectangular patch of orchids the size of a nineteenth century man.

Nova barked well down below us. She'd found another bear. This one she sent up a hickory tree, and it gawked at us from high on the trunk. Now she had two of them to keep in the air like a vaudevillian spinning plates. She circled and yapped while we counted grave markers. Ethan snapped pictures to show his grandmother, and Billy made me eat a sumac seed against my will.

That was one of my more satisfying afternoons as I look back on it now. A walk in the woods with people I liked and a dog that I adored. A visit to a place so oddly lovely that it left us all unsettled. Then we met up at the pizza shack down in Crozet proper while Nova slept in the truck. Not the pretentious lousy pizza place where all the Charlottesvillians eat but the shabby one where the pies are good and the cops all come for lunch.

That was my final leisurely afternoon before the McShanes showed up. Michael always arrived with a project in mind. This time his heart was set on plank fencing. We already had it along the boundary where the estate met the road, and the run of it nearest the

blacktop had been knocked down twice already. Once by
a texting sober teenaged girl in a yellow Mustang and
once by a Breedlove full of Ancient Age in a panel truck.
I'd made the repairs, and I kept the fence sparkling
white, which was all good and well for road frontage.
Running the stuff across the back pasture seemed to me
the construction equivalent of dumping your money in a
pile and setting it on fire.

Michael took my point, but the chef had mentioned
to Michael's wife how happy the sight of plank fencing
out the kitchen window would make him. There was a
stretch of wire fence beyond the barn he could see when
he stood at the sink, and he'd suggested he'd be more
inspired by planking.

"Why don't we run it just where he can see it?" I
suggested to Michael, but his native compulsiveness
kicked in. He informed me he wouldn't feel right with a
rigged solution like that.

So I went to the builder's supply and bought enough
fence posts to get us started, and Michael even stayed
with the job for three legitimate days. Then something
went haywire on the Nikkei, and Michael retired to his
study. After that he got busy revarnishing his wet bar
and weeding the vegetable garden. He'd come check on
me every now and again without offering any help.

It's a two-man job. Partly because you need the
extra hands for it, and partly because there's an awful lot
of misery to go around. I called Ethan to see if he
wanted to work. He was picking up part time money at
his father's law firm in Richmond where, to hear it from
him, he pushed mail around on a cart two times a day. I
told him he could work when he wanted and visit his
grandmother whenever he liked. That suited Ethan right
down to the ground.

Ethan came early the day the McShanes were due to
head back to Texas. He parked his beat up coupe at my
house, and me and him and Nova went bouncing across
the pasture in my truck. I'd started with the run of fence
I knew the chef could see, a thirty yard section I'd not
only built but had already painted.

I'd strung a line and hammered stakes in where the new fenceposts would go. I backed up the tractor and augered a hole so Ethan could see how to do it. He'd never been on a tractor before, and he was fearful there at first. So I shared with Ethan my core beliefs. It didn't take long since I've only got two. "Everybody ought to get arrested once, especially cops and judges, and everybody needs to know how to drive a tractor in a pinch."

I sent Ethan on a loop out across the field so he could learn the gears, and it was like he'd been perched on a tractor seat his whole life after that.

We shoved posts in at a decent clip. The herd wandered over to watch us, but they could see Nova studying them and doing her collie math, so they hung back except for the odd bull calf that Nova would intercept. We lunched in the shade of the barn on saltines, pickles, and potted meat.

Ethan told me all about Hattie's husband, who he'd known as Grandpa Buck. Buck had been a timber speculator and a commercial builder. He'd gone crabbing in the Chesapeake and had fallen out of his boat. Somebody came across it a good twenty-four hours later. They never saw Grandpa Buck again.

"Gom hasn't been the same after that."

"Guess not."

"Not like she is now -- forgetful and stuff -- but like somebody turned her volume down."

"They married forever?"

Ethan nodded. He thought it was fifty-eight years.

"Kind of hard to know what to be up to after that."

Michael drove his Gator up to see us in his usual breakneck sort of way.

"Looking good," he told us.

I made a proper introduction to Ethan. It seemed to me Michael was just the sort of fellow Ethan needed to know. Michael was enormously successful and fabulously rich but had managed somehow to avoid being a jackass.

"We're heading out," he told me, meaning back to Texas.

I suddenly felt like a kid whose parents were going on vacation. Not that Michael meddled and made anything especially difficult for me, but once they'd flown off I could be sure nobody was watching from the house. Contemplating projects. Making bathtubs overflow. I'd go back to having a vacant showplace to curate and demouse.

"They kind of set fire to the sink," Michael told me as a parting shot.

I nodded and told Michael just, "All right."

That's why me and Michael got along. He could tell me they'd set the sink on fire, flooded the upstairs hallway, pulled a chandelier out of the ceiling, shattered the sliding door, and I'd only ever tell him, "All right." Then he'd come back from Texas and find everything in order.

Me and Ethan and Nova watched him tear back across the pasture at full throttle. He endured a few jolts along the way that made my kidneys hurt.

We were two weeks putting that fence up, worked almost to September. Ethan would show up early. He got to where he would drive the tractor out of the barn. I gave him a few pointers and turned him loose to learn what to do on his own. Since I wasn't his father, I could manage that without any anguish to speak of. Ethan was a conscientious, careful kid. He drove the tractor at a funereal pace. Never pried with my shovel handle. Seemed to love my dog like I did. And every day at three he'd clean up at the spigot behind the big house, climb in his battered coupe, and drive up to see his Gom.

Then school started for Ethan, and me and Nova were left to paint the new fence alone. In truth, the dog wasn't awfully much help unless getting splattered counts. I found it difficult painting a thing just belted Galloways would see.

X

September was high grass season up at Evergreen. I had to mow once every eight or nine days just to stay ahead of things, and there seemed to be a general uneasiness among the patient population, a communal upset about the prospect of leaving the lawn and getting driven indoors by autumn.

The patients up there were funny that way. They were like a school of fish. One of them would get alarmed and take a turn, and the rest of them usually followed. So the staff was always fighting to keep agitation from gaining a foothold.

They couldn't do much about the sundowning. That's just a fact of nursing home life. I'd been up there an evening or two when I'd started late on mowing, and sunset had a way of stirring the patients up. Even the undemented ones would get confused and exasperated. People who'd been sane in the afternoon would go off the rails come twilight. It was weird to watch and seemed about as immutable as the moon and tides.

Talking to them helped a little. I was walking with Agatha as she steered Arthur Bigelow inside late one afternoon when the sun was low behind the trees and the shadows had gotten long. Arthur grew irate and tearful, close to abusive in a matter of minutes. Suddenly, nothing suited him and everything was wrong. He cried about buddies he'd lost in the service, was angry at his wife who Arthur insisted was coming to pick him up soon. He told us the doctors operated on him almost every night.

"Especially that one," he said and pointed at a rhododendron by the parking lot.

It was strange to watch Arthur dip in and out of his proper senses. Chiefly, he seemed overwhelmingly sad to have arrived where he'd ended up. Not at Evergreen but just old and tired, bereft of family and friends, and with nothing to do but wait for time to pass and life to end.

Somehow twilight brought all of it bubbling to the surface. It was the very stuff I think about in the middle of the night when the moon wakes me up or a rafter pops or the wind tries all the windows. I'll lay there sifting through my antagonisms and regrets. I just don't have a cane to wave or tomato paste can internals.

After a few minutes in his room, with the lights turned up and the bed turned down, Arthur became lucid again. It wasn't as if he all at once woke up to who he was. He simply shifted from weepy and befuddled to his usual brand of grumpy.

The transition was so seamless that I wasn't sure he'd changed until he poked me and asked, "Why in the world would you cut grass this time of day?"

That evening shook me up a little. Not just Arthur specifically but the thoroughgoing uproar of the place. The demented patients had gotten frantic. The normal ones were acting unhinged. Agatha and Matt and Denise and a couple of orderlies were working to calm them all down. It looked to me like a close thing for probably half an hour. Then the sun dipped low, it got proper dark, and general fatigue settled in.

The staff was clearly outnumbered and overwhelmed, at least for that part of the day. They'd had a couple of patients take advantage of the bedlam by slipping away to roam off the grounds. With everybody present raising such a ruckus, it wouldn't be much of a chore for a wandering patient to go unmissed for a while.

They hadn't lost anybody for four or five years, not since a gentleman who'd been found by a family from Ohio. They'd come across him out at an overlook on the parkway in his housecoat and slippers. He'd been carrying with him just a buffalo nickel and a spoon. He didn't know where he was going and couldn't recall where he'd come from. The truth was he'd walked no more than fifty yards straight through the woods just as the sun was sinking and the uproar had begun.

My experience up at Evergreen -- about as well run as a place like that could be -- had left me to wonder why patients didn't disappear routinely. A mislaid inmate every five years or so seemed a miracle to me.

So I wasn't too surprised when a patient disappeared. I was right there when it happened with my herding dog at my side, and neither one of us knew we'd let one get away until Matt told us.

"Where did she go? She was right here."

"Where did who go?" I asked him.

"You know." He held his hand out maybe five and a half feet off the ground.

"Oh. Her."

Matt was immune to sarcasm. Everything sounded the same to him, so he just stood there waiting for me to name the creature he'd described.

"Who are we talking about?" I finally asked him.

He held his hand out again. "You know. Ethan's . . .," and he trailed off. Matt wasn't the sort to finish strong when mumbling was an option.

"Mrs. Womble?"

He nodded. "They told me she was out here with you."

Of course, nobody had told Matt any such thing. That was just his way of shaping reality to suit him. How could he have lost Mrs. Womble if she was out in the yard with me?

"She's no speed burner," I told him. "She's bound to be around here somewhere."

I'd like to say Nova and I helped Matt look for Hattie around the grounds, but he just stayed where he was while me and Nova circulated. Everybody had long been inside by then, and I had to think Hattie was in the TV room or the dining hall. Out of the patients I knew, she seemed the least likely to lose her bearings and just wander off.

We rejoined Matt where we'd left him. "She's not out here."

He exhaled again.

"She's probably inside somewhere," I suggested. "Maybe you just missed her."

Matt checked his phone. He read a text. He chuckled. He'd started in on a response when I reached over and removed the thing from his hands. He blew another breath and glared at me with teenaged consternation.

"Go have a look," I told him.

He went inside. I imagined him skulking through the place. Resenting me. Resenting Hattie Womble. Pausing in the TV room to watch a little Andy Griffith.

Nobody panicked. That was what impressed me right away. Well, nobody panicked except for Matt a little. He was mostly upset because he didn't think he should be blamed for losing Mrs. Womble, not that anybody had gone to the bother to blame him. Everybody else was scouring the place in a systematic fashion while Matt devoted himself to building a case that I'd seen Mrs. Womble last.

I'd talked to her. I remembered that. I'd sat for a while with Hattie and Ethan. They were going on about fall foliage while Hattie's hand rested on Nova's head. This is part of the world people flock to once the leaves have turned, and Ethan and Hattie were describing their favorite leaf peeper panoramas. One of Hattie's was close by, straight through the woods near the overlook where the previous wayward patient had been found. Since all of the official employees had their procedures and their duties, that left only me and Nova free to go play the hunch I had.

I fetched my flashlight out the truck, crossed the lawn and entered the woods. I followed a deer path as far as it went and then blazed a trail through the brush. Nova followed close behind me, and when we flushed a pair of quails, we talked each other out of heart attacks.

There was just a band of forest where I was, a spot where Blue Ridge Parkway right of way butted against the Evergreen property line. I knew we'd come to the grassy boundary of the roadway in due time, and I had a light and proper shoes and a dog for company. Even still, it was a bit unnerving to blunder through the woods in the dark. It hardly seemed the sort of thing Ethan's grandmother would get up to. I shined my flashlight around and examined what of the forest the beam would reach, but I hardly expected to find Hattie Womble out in the scrub somewhere.

At the overlook, I peered down over the rock retaining wall. There was maybe a forty foot drop, but I didn't see anything other than twelve-pack boxes and scattershot rotting trash. The main view was south and a little west, towards Wintergreen and Lynchburg. Turning east, all I could see was wooded upslope and unpeopled national park. This wasn't the territory for a little old lady in flats and a denim skirt.

"She's not out here," I told Nova. "They've probably found her already."

I knew I was wrong when I came out of the woods and saw Mr. Borland crossing the main lawn at a trot.

I'd only spoken with him a time or two. He ran the place for a holding company located in D. C.. Mr. Borland kept Evergreen duly licensed and up to exacting standards. He was a numbers cruncher but also a decent sort. He frequently circulated among the clients (he called them) to make sure they were content, and Agatha thought well of him, which was endorsement enough for me.

They were still counting heads inside, and they'd switched all the floodlights on. Matt and one of the orderlies -- a night-shifter I didn't know -- were calling for Mrs. Womble and tromping through the shrubbery. Denise was looking for her in her ashtray corner of the lot. Mr. Borland circled round to make sure she wasn't hiding on the air conditioner slab.

I played my light beam around the perimeter of the lawn, but I can't say I expected to find Hattie Womble in the bushes. I even began to wonder if Ethan might have taken her for a ride.

"I'm told you talked with her," Mr. Borland said, still out of breath from jogging across the lawn.

"Yes sir." He was probably younger than me, and he'd invited me to call him Hank, but he was far too buttoned-down and business-like for that sort of thing.

"Did she seem . . . upset? Confused?"

I shook my head. "She was talking with her grandson. Have you met Ethan?"

Mr. Borland nodded.

"They were sitting over there chatting." I pointed to Mrs. Womble's usual chair by the rose of Sharon bush.

"Was she unhappy?"

"No sir. We were all talking about autumn coming on. She was looking forward to the leaves."

"Hmm," Mr. Borland told me. He seemed entirely out of his element, was far better with a ledger than with people. I hated to see him so troubled and uneasy and wanted to help him any way I could.

"I'm wondering if maybe Ethan left and took his grandmother with him?"

"Would he do that?" Mr. Borland asked me.

I shrugged. "I'm guessing he'd tell somebody first. I know him pretty well. I doubt he'd just pack her off in his car and leave. But maybe wires got crossed somewhere. That would make the most sense to me."

"Did Mrs. Womble's grandson talk to you?" Mr. Borland called out to Matt.

Matt was standing in a shaft of floodlight, so I could see his gears turning. Who's Mrs. Womble? Which one's her grandson? Why would he talk to me? Matt lumbered through his catalog of possibilities. He finally said to Mr. Borland, "What?"

"Ethan would have said something to Agatha. Maybe even Denise. Easiest thing would be if I just called him."

Mr. Borland's hand shot out, and he grabbed my forearm hard. "And tell him what?"

"Oh, right," I said. I thought for a moment, settled on a plan, and then went ahead and called up Ethan. Mr. Borland stood by anxiously and watched.

"Hey, it's me," I told him. "You want to work on Saturday?"

Ethan reminded me that we'd already set up Saturday work.

"Yeah, of course. And I've got some pay for you. You visiting Hattie tomorrow?"

Ethan couldn't remember any money I owed him, and of course he was visiting his grandmother like he always did.

"All right, buddy. We'll straighten it out." I signed off and hung up. "Wherever she went, it wasn't with him," I told Mr. Borland. "I'd be shocked if she's not inside some place."

"Well get ready, sugar," Denise said as she came up behind us. She'd passed out of her corner of the lot and back in through the building. She'd reconnoitered before she'd ventured across the lawn to tell us, "That woman just ain't nowhere at all."

Mr. Borland had company protocol to follow. He knew once he brought the local police in and alerted the family, nothing good for Evergreen was likely to transpire. If Mrs. Womble turned up hurt or dead, that'd be a terrible state of affairs. There'd be lawsuits and wretched press. Most of the patients would probably go elsewhere.

Even if they found Mrs. Womble in pristine shape, that would be a bad thing too. A nursing home that lets a patient wander off into the woods is just a pack of coyotes away from a gruesome fatality.

So it was a freighted moment when Agatha came out to report that they'd scoured the building and Mrs. Womble wasn't anywhere at all. We all detailed the last time we'd seen her. Where she'd been and how she'd looked. What, in my case, she had said as a measure of her thinking.

"She seemed . . . fine," I told them, and I asked of Agatha, "You've checked every little where?"

She nodded, and Mr. Borland sagged a little and said, "Well."

He'd turned to go to his office, to make the call that might spoil the place, when I asked him if he'd hold up for a minute. "I know a guy. Let me call him and see if he can give us a hand."

Mr. Borland was guarded but agreeable. I didn't have Officer Crocker's number, but I found him listed in the phonebook inside at the nurse's station. His wife answered, and I felt compelled, the way I sometimes do, to over explain just who I was and why precisely I was calling.

She lost interest and shouted, "Eddie." Officer T. E. Crocker picked up.

He remembered me even before I'd finished reminding him who I was.

"How did your dog make out?" he asked me, and I told him about her stick and her nicked up liver.

"Isn't that something," he said, "but I don't guess that's why you're calling."

"We've got kind of a problem out here in Afton. I was hoping you could help."

The thing I found out about Officer Crocker was that he required, as a general rule, a lot less explaining than I was willing to subject him to. He came straight out to Evergreen in his cruiser but dressed in civilian clothes. Nova ran over to greet him like she knew he needed a dog Hello.

I introduced him to Mr. Borland straightaway, but "Officer Crocker" wouldn't do. He stuck out his hand and told Mr. Borland, "Eddie." Then he added right behind it, "I can give you a couple of hours, but then we'll have to call this in."

Eddie got all the particulars from the gang of us out there. He recognized that Agatha was talking the purest sense and closed the rest of us off so he could pump her for what she had on Mrs. Womble. Then he had her tour him through the building and show him all the closets and cubbies. At his request, Agatha brought out the snapshot of Mrs. Womble from her file. She was a shrunken white-haired lady in a place overrun with them.

When they came back out, we all gathered on the lawn where the floodlights were brightest. Eddie told us how he thought we ought to search.

Eddie wanted us spiraling out in an organized way. Of course, only me and him had working flashlights. Mr. Borland found one in his office drawer that was about the size of a pencil, and the orderly -- Dwayne was his name -- fished a nine-volt out of his car. The beam was yellow for about a minute, and then there was no beam at all.

I gave Matt and Dwayne my light. We sent Mr. Borland down the drive, and me and Eddie and Nova plunged into the woods. Agatha and Denise stayed behind to keep tabs on everybody else.

It was more than a little tough out there without a light in hand. Eddie would play his beam around in an organized sort of way, and he tried to be mindful of where I might be stepping, but he couldn't worry about where I put my feet as much as I could.

It didn't help that he told me, "Got to watch for copperheads."

I was puckered enough to know that I was mindful of them already, just waiting to feel the ropy length of one of them under foot. As it was, we spooked a good dozen deer and put an owl to flight. We could hear coyotes off to the north, and Eddie picked up the screech of a bobcat. Everything was conspiring out there to tell us how wild a place it was.

"A night in the woods," Eddie told me, "in this kind of weather doesn't seem like much of a trial until you get out here and see what's going on."

"Yeah," was all I could manage.

"Is she a tough old lady?"

"I guess. Never struck me as the outdoorsy sort."

Nova stuck with us for the most part, except when deer proved a bit too tempting for her. Even then, she'd dart out at them in full yelp and come straight back. We popped out of the woods just south of the overlook. We checked a stretch of road down that way and then turned around and walked back to the overlook lot. There were a couple of guys sitting on the hood of a Camaro. They were drinking bargain beer and throwing their cans down in the woods.

It was pleasing, in an otherwise fraught situation, to watch Eddie handle those fellows.

"Have you seen anybody around here on foot?" he asked them. "An older woman maybe?"

"Who wants to know?" the one in the filthier coveralls asked him back. Then he emptied his beer, crushed his can, and threw it over the fieldstone overlook wall.

"All right, boys," Eddie said, and he brought out a badge in a leather wallet. "These next few minutes might matter for you a little more than you'd hoped."

"Hell, man. Why didn't you say you was a cop?" the slightly cleaner and skinnier one asked of Eddie.

"We ain't done nothing," the one in the coveralls barked.

"This isn't about you. We're looking for a woman. She's old and she's lost and on foot. Seen anybody like that?"

"Hadn't seen nobody."

This time the wiry one slugged his beer down and sent his can sailing into the woods. That was all Eddie could stand.

"License and registration," Eddie said as he reached over and grabbed the twelve pack that was resting between those fellows on the hood.

Those boys had a back-hollow moment between them when they were forced to decide if they wanted to do what Eddie was asking or simply fight instead. It was an interesting thing to see from a lawful civilian point of view. Those boys clearly were torn between getting a fine or a felony conviction. The first one would be cheaper but the other one more fun.

That's when Nova stepped in to straighten things out. I'd never even heard her growl, so I didn't know what the sound was at first. Since she was slightly in front of me, I couldn't see her exposed teeth, but I could tell by the way she was watching those boys that she meant serious canine business. They'd probably kicked enough dogs around between them to know it as well.

"Call him off," the one in the coveralls said. He reached around and fished out his wallet. "Registration's in the glovebox somewhere."

"Get it," Eddie told him.

I guess Nova felt the atmosphere go slack because she dropped the growl, smacked her lips, and glanced my way sheepishly. Her looked seemed to tell me, "I'm

sorry you had to see that, but you know how crackers
are."

In addition to the license and the registration, Eddie
took that fellow's key as well.

"Call somebody to pick you up," Eddie told them
both. "Neither one of you is fit to drive."

When they protested they couldn't call anybody,
didn't have any friends at all, Eddie just said to them,
"Imagine that."

He stepped over to the wall and shined his light
down at the rubbish. "You come back tomorrow, clean
this mess up, and we'll see about your car."

"How are we supposed to get home!?" The wiry
one hit a note that brought another growl out of Nova.
"All right. All right," he told her, and those boys struck
out south along the parkway, slogging along on foot.
Long after the darkness had swallowed them up, we
could still hear them swearing and burping.

Eddie swept his light up and down the road. Nova
nosed his trouser leg. He scratched her ears, told her,
"Good girl."

We cut back through the woods about one hundred
yards north of where we'd come out. We took our time
and searched the brush everywhere Eddie's beam would
reach. We found a raccoon and a turtle about the size of
a dinner plate, but there wasn't any sign of Hattie
Womble. When we came back out of the woods, we
could see Matt and Dwayne and Mr. Borland all waiting
for us in the lot. They looked to have had as much luck
as we did.

"What's your procedure?" Eddie asked Mr. Borland.

"County police, state police, and family. In that
order."

"I'll bring in the county. You call Richmond. Let's
hold off on the family until we get it all in place."

"We ought to tell Ethan," I said to Mr. Borland. I
told Eddie. "Her grandson. He's out here every day.
Knows more about her than the rest of us put together."

"Can you keep it just him?" Eddie asked me.

I thought I could and told him as much.

XI

She hadn't said a thing to him, Ethan told us. He'd
left her sitting in her favorite chair. Ethan and I were
standing right beside it at the time, and he rested his
hand on the arched back as he spoke.

He'd raced straight out to Evergreen. Since his
parents were dining with friends in Charlottesville, he
hadn't needed to tell them a thing.

"She didn't seem . . . down?" Mr. Borland asked.

Ethan shook his head. "Gom is . . ." He looked to
me for help.

"Realistic?" I suggested.

"Yeah," Ethan said. "Exactly. She's lost Grandpa
Buck. She's sold her house. She's been sick off and on
for years. Her friends are mostly dead. And she's
confused sometimes, but she's not half as down as I'd
be."

The officials all came rolling in over the next hour.
A couple of county policemen, fellows Eddie knew and
trusted. Four state troopers from the barracks in the
valley. A park service ranger named Tony, in case she
happened to have gotten that far. Then trouble arrived
in the person of Captain Frank L. Stenson of the
Virginia State Police. He was wearing an olive drab
jumpsuit with his name on a pocket flap and his stripes
on a sleeve. His pant legs were tucked into what
appeared to be paratrooper boots. He'd brought two
assistants in his unmarked sedan. One of them was
young and ambitious, alert and attentive and well-
scrubbed. The other one was about my age, and he
looked more than a little worn down.

The cause for it became evident soon enough.
Every time Captain Frank L. Stenson needed anything at

all, he turned to his older assistant and barked out what he wanted.

Douglas (the gentleman's name was) would say, "Right, Frank L.," and get it done. Sometimes it was official state police business. Sometimes it was an Almond Joy straight out of the glovebox. Captain Frank L. Stenson appeared to live on cups of plain hot water and Almond Joys.

The younger assistant's name was Tad or Tod, depending on what Frank L. Stenson deigned to call him. He lingered at the captain's elbow. Confirmed the captain's suspicions. Congratulated the captain on his piercing insights. Repeated to Douglas most everything the captain asked him to do.

They both called him Frank L., though it sounded like Frankel. Nobody else called him anything because he avoided truck with civilians. If we wanted to bring an item to Captain Frank L. Stenson's attention, we had to share it with Tad/Tod who would then decide what of it Frankel needed to hear.

The only thing Frank L. Stenson said directly to me throughout the whole ordeal came about two minutes after he'd rolled up in his sedan. He took one look at Nova, who was sitting close beside me, and he announced in his Foghorn Leghorn way, "I don't much care for dogs."

Immediately thereafter, Tad/Tod approached us and said to me and Nova together, "Frankel would prefer if you'd shut your dog away, perhaps in your car."

"When exactly," I asked Tad/Tod, "did I start working for Frankel?"

So I got iced out immediately by Captain Stenson and his boys, and Eddie got shoved aside as well because he was wearing civies. We watched the captain tour the grounds in search of a suitable spot for a command center. He selected a location out in the middle of the lawn and then instructed Tad/Tod to set up his tent, which Tad/Tod passed on to Douglas.

Douglas looked so weary that me and Eddie threw in to give him a hand.

At this point, Captain Frank L. Stenson still knew nothing about Hattie Womble. He was into his second Almond Joy and his third cup of hot water before he barked directly at Douglas, "Where's my profile of the victim?"

"Victim?" Ethan said.

"Who are you?" Captain Stenson asked.

"Victim's grandson, sir," Tad/Tod told him.

"She's probably right around here somewhere. Just wandered off," Ethan said.

"That's the spirit," Frank L. Stenson told Ethan and gave him a theatrical slap on the back.

Among the people attached to Evergreen and the ones who'd shown up to help look for Hattie Womble, Frank L. Stenson let it be known that he only approved of Mr. Borland. Like the captain, Mr. Borland was an orderly sort of guy with a taste for channels and procedure and an innate understanding of the importance of rank and command control in such an undertaking. It didn't hurt that Mr. Borland called Frank L. Stenson "Captain, sir."

Eddie lingered for a bit but then headed home to sleep before his shift. He gave me his card so I could call him if we needed his help before dawn. Tony the ranger produced a topographical map of the area. Frank L. Stenson spread it out on a folding table Douglas had fetched from the trunk of their sedan. He was quick to say he didn't like the scale of Tony's map, and him and Tad/Tod passed a quarter hour pinpointing where we were.

Tony kept offering to show them but the captain wouldn't allow it. He declared it was a jurisdictional sort of thing. They finally settled on a spot a good half mile from where they were standing.

"All right, then," he said as if the program was now officially underway.

I motioned for Ethan to follow me to the building. I knew he'd want the satisfaction of looking around inside, so me and Agatha took him in and let him search the place on his own. Most of the patients were asleep by then. It was crowding eleven o'clock. Dozens of TV

sets were still playing throughout the place. Hattie
Womble's room was tidy. Her bed was turned down, but
she clearly wasn't anywhere to be seen. Agatha even
unlocked the basement door so we could take a look.
Just service panels. Folding chairs. A couple of busted
hospital beds.

I suggested to Ethan that me and him ride around
the area, go anywhere Hattie might have reached on foot.
That seemed agreeable to him, so we went back outside.
Nova wasn't by the door where I'd left her. I could hear
her barking at me, but she sounded muffled and shut
away. It took me a moment to find her in the back of
one of the state police cruisers. I would have had a lively
word with Captain Frank L. Stenson, but Ethan's parents
had gotten a call from Mr. Borland and had rolled up to
Evergreen by then.

Ethan's father was going off like only a Richmond
lawyer can. Ethan's mother was more mousy than I
would have predicted. Whenever she'd try to say
something to Dwight he'd show her the palm of his
hand.

Douglas told me, "Sorry," as he let Nova out of the
cruiser. "Frankel got bit by a bomb dog once. Soured
him on the things."

That, of course, was the moment my Chevy chose
not to start. It turned over and coughed and quit, and
then the battery dragged and waned, which is how we
ended up in Ethan's coupe. It turned out the interior of
Ethan's car was the only teenaged thing about him. That
coupe was like a laundry hamper on wheels. Nova rode
on top of a welter of sweatshirts and jeans heaped on
the backseat while I shared my floorboard with three
pairs of sneakers.

Ethan's dash lights were all out. His headlights only
brightened up when the engine revved, and Ethan did an
awful lot of steering for a guy negotiating a straight
driveway. He was nervous and upset and had kept it
bottled up until we were out on the Afton road, away
from Evergreen and his parents.

"I'm scared for her," he told me. "She doesn't like the dark. She's got cataracts and can't see like she used to."

"She probably just took a wrong turn and couldn't make her way back."

There are paths all over the place in the forest up around Afton. Old logging roads and horse trails, the Appalachian Trail itself with its numerous side routes to peaks and camping sheds and overlooks. So there was a whole network of byways that wound around and intersected. Even in daylight without cataracts, you could get back in the woods and spend a full day trying to get out.

This was near midnight, and we were hunting an octogenarian who could only half see. So even though I kept asking myself, "Where would I be if I were Hattie?" the only answer that made sense was "back at Evergreen in bed."

We parked in a roadside pullout on the Blue Ridge Parkway. Ethan had a flashlight in his trunk that lasted about six minutes. By then, mine was starting to look a little played out as well. Fortunately for us, the moon had risen, and it was nearly full, so once my light had died, we found we could see just fine without it.

A doe tried to cross the road ahead of us, and Nova charged up to correct it. She spied another one well up beyond it and went running after that one as well. I didn't worry about her much on the Parkway. It was so lightly traveled at this time of night to be little short of desolate. All grassy shoulder and decorative rail fencing, the odd cement milepost sign. We walked right down the middle of the road for a considerable while and only had to move once to let an RV lumber by.

When we came to a parking lot at a trailhead near the turn to the old Howardsville Road, we ventured into the forest for a while. We'd been calling for Hattie every few minutes or so all along. It had sounded all right in the roadway but was unnerving in the woods.

"Have they ever lost anybody before?" Ethan wanted to know.

"A guy walked off a few years back. They found him at an overlook."

Except for the occasion, we would have been having a fine enough time in the woods. Ethan was an easy kid to walk along and chat with, and the moonlight was washing through the canopy in a dazzling sort of way. You could have read a phonebook there in the forest in that ravishing, blue-tinted glow. Anything that wasn't green and leafy shone like it was phosphorescent. Ethan was wearing a white t-shirt, and I could have seen him a half mile away.

We were exceedingly hopeful still. Ours isn't a killing wilderness. The coyotes will linger if you're failing, and the buzzards will gnaw on you once you're dead, but it was a warm autumn night, and a woman strong enough to wander could be out in those woods for a great while without meeting any harm. Primarily, me and Ethan were wondering together where Hattie might have gone and why she'd chosen this evening to go there.

"She didn't say anything out of the way at all?"

I could see Ethan replaying the afternoon's conversation in his head. "We talked a little about your place. I told her I was helping you with your fence."

"What did she say about that?"

"She seemed to be curious about the cellar. Wanted to know if I'd been down there. Something about the structural beams."

So I decided in that instant that Harriet Womble was on her way to the basement of the McShane's estate house because she'd gotten it in her head that she needed to see the timbers of the place firsthand.

"If that's not where she is, it sure might be where she's going. Let's give it a look," I said to Ethan, and that buoyed us quite a lot. We didn't care anymore about the sticks and the roots along the trail. We just went flying out of the woods with Nova nipping and herding us some, and we made for Ethan's battered coupe at a run.

We came down off the mountain on the old Rockfish Gap Turnpike. We stopped at the pullout where the trucks cooled their brakes and where I'd bought my shrimp. There was a tractor trailer idling in there with its amber running lights lit. I mounted the running board, knocked on the side glass, and got sworn at prodigiously.

The driver had been stretched out in his bunk asleep.

"I've got a gun," he told me.

"You won't need it. We're just looking for a woman."

"Try the motel down in Greenwood. I ain't got nobody up here."

"Not that kind of woman. An older woman. Lives up at the nursing home."

"Haven't seen nobody like that."

His window had only been open a crack, and he finally rolled it all the way down.

"I've been asleep for a couple of hours, wouldn't have seen her go by."

I went ahead and allowed that fact to shore up my theory a little, and I returned to Ethan's coupe more confident than I had any right to be.

"He didn't see her, but he was sleeping. I've got a feeling she's headed to the house."

That was the most profound difference between me and Captain Stenson and the reason he was better suited for this sort of thing than I was. I allowed myself to be fueled by hunches and driven by intuition while Frank L. Stenson's only "feeling" was an unnatural fear of dogs.

There I'd thought he was a fool for being businesslike and antiseptic, figured all my dashing around was better suited to our goal. Running down to the McShane's house was all about me getting out and doing something. Captain Stenson knew enough to stay where he was and think it through. I came to all of this only at length after quite a lot of dashing around.

We piled out of Ethan's car by the McShane's woodshed and just stood there and called for Hattie. We both expected to hear her call back. I unlocked the house without looking around to see where she might have gone in. We passed through towards the basement door, shouting her name out every few steps. Halfway down the stairs, I thought I heard her speak, but it was just the treads creaking and the echo from the cellar.

There were only three bare bulbs down there and a lot of gloomy, unlit cellar. I plugged in a droplight Michael had left in a tangle of cord on the lid of the chest freezer. That allowed us at least to study the timbers Hattie Womble had spoken of and might have wished to see.

I'd never paid any notice to them before that night with Ethan. Each of them measured about ten by ten, and they spanned the entire cellar. They supported the house so thoroughly that posts were few and far between. The odd thing was those timbers weren't, in fact, just timbers at all. They were lapped and pegged and cunningly fitted together every which way like something on the order of eighteenth-century handworked lamination.

Now that I was looking at them with purpose and attention, I knew I'd never seen their like before.

"What did she tell you about them?" I asked of Ethan while fingering an impeccable timber joint.

"I was telling her about a desk I had made about of that wood-chip junk."

"Particle board?"

"Yeah, but worse, like it's waiting to be sawdust. And she got reminded of these," Ethan told me. "She's big on craftsmanship."

Just then Nova gave a yip. She was off in a gloomy corner of the basement, and I went marching over with the droplight. Nova was peering behind the furnace. I had a little jolt of hope that we'd find Hattie Womble lurking back there. No such luck.

"Oh," I said when I saw him stretched full out on the cement. "Howard."

He was digesting a mouse or chipmunk and didn't appear to have been long at it. Ethan squeezed in for a look. "Howard?" was all he said.

Back outside, Ethan slid his seat forward to let Nova onto his heap of clothes.

"My dad might even be finished yelling by now."

That struck me as optimistic.

XII

Ethan was right in a fashion. Dwight had finished yelling at Mr. Borland and had turned his fury instead on the staff. Especially Agatha. Of course, she was the one he had no cause at all to rage at. Agatha was always attentive and conscientious. There just wasn't enough of her to go around. Denise and Matt did as little as they could, while the orderlies and nurses had their hands full with those patients in no condition to venture out in the yard and sit in the sun.

But Ethan's father was both incensed and trained as an attorney, so he had a lot to say about who was going to get destroyed and how.

Every now and again his wife would touch his sleeve and tell him, "Dwight," in a voice so low and tentative she sounded like a frog.

"Dwight. Dwight. Dwight."

She was usually four or five Dwights in before he'd turn on her and snap, "What?!"

She'd burble some calming suggestion, and he'd jerk his arm away.

Dwight had long since become invisible to Captain Frank L. Stenson who had dispatched his state policemen to cover all the local roadways. They were cruising the county routes with their spotlights on, and the captain had called in a chopper from Richmond which was already flying over the southern end of the national park.

When Tad/Tod attempted to explain the science of infrared scanners to Dwight and speak to him of the grid their helicopter was flying, Dwight heard him out for a nanosecond before telling him, "Shut up!"

I felt a little sorry for Tad/Tod and asked him what Ethan and I could do. I told him where we'd been and shared with him a couple of my hunches. I assured him we stood ready to go anywhere we could be of help.

Tad/Tod glanced at Nova and acquainted me again with Captain Frank L. Stenson's poor opinion of dogs. Then he handed me Frank L.'s cup and said, "Plain hot water, from the tap."

It sounded like Captain Stenson was in radio contact with police and park officials all over the place. He insisted on over-the-air updates every quarter hour, so people were checking in incessantly telling him what they hadn't found. Everybody up at Evergreen was angry or exhausted except for Agatha who looked stricken to me. Mr. Borland looked stricken as well, but his was more a fiduciary upset. Agatha was worried about Hattie Womble out in this dark world alone.

I put my arm around her and squired her away from the command center, away from the crackling walkie-talkie voices with nothing to report. Agatha was cursed with a strenuously overactive imagination, so she was picturing Ethan's grandmother in all manner of distress. Stalked by bears. Surrounded by wolves. Snatched off the road by lawless hillbillies.

"They would have seen her by now if she was just walking along," Agatha insisted.

Agatha stayed busy regretting everything she hadn't done to close off the opportunity for Hattie Womble to wander. That was the sort of exercise that would never occur to Denise or Matt. By now they'd both asked Mr. Borland if they'd get paid for a double shift.

It took us a good half hour before we made a dent in Agatha, before we managed to convince her that on a warm night in a benign part of the world, even a woman as old and frail and occasionally addled as Mrs. Womble was more likely than not to be just fine once the morning light had come. Agatha was prepared to hope we were possibly right but not, at that moment, ready to believe it with any conviction. That's just when Ethan's father wandered over to yell at her.

"Dad," Ethan told him. "Dad. Dad." He was his mother's son. He even touched his father's sleeve.

I grabbed Dwight fully by the arm with both of my hands together. I walked him away from Agatha so we could have the sort of chat that looks civilized, even cordial, from a distance.

"Let me tell you . . ." he started but I persuaded him to fall silent by squeezing shut the veins that carried blood below his elbow.

"No," I said, and glanced towards Ethan and Agatha, smiling so they wouldn't think anything amiss. "Let me tell you."

By then all Dwight could manage was a pained wince and an "Ouch."

Once he'd promised he'd stand by quietly while I explained a few things to him, I let his blood flow again but kept a grip on him nonetheless. Nova had followed us across the lawn and was smiling up at Dwight. I was wearing a grin myself. He must have thought we were demonic. All I know is he got unlawyerly in a hurry and stayed that way the whole time that I talked.

I can't be sure he wasn't busy calculating ways to sue me, but he did let me tell him how my affection for his mother was only rivaled by my fondness for his son. I assured him I'd be as upset as he was if I thought the staff had neglected Hattie, and then I pointed at Agatha. "She's the last one you ought to complain about."

I cataloged Agatha's virtues for Dwight. I told him if he wanted to be litigious, he ought to sue the people who owned the place for economizing on staff. "None of those guys are here," I told him. "Isn't that always the way?" Then I gave him the brand of slap on the back Captain Frank L. Stenson favored.

Ethan's father looked from me to Nova. She was still smiling at his feet. "Who are you again?" he finally asked.

By sunrise we didn't know any more than we had known at midnight. Mrs. Womble was gone as if she'd evaporated. Officer Crocker came rolling back into the lot around seven, and Tad/Tod put a call in to the Richmond police academy to see if they had a busload of cadets they could spare for the search. By then the helicopter had landed on a fairway at the Swannanoa

Golf Club. They had a best ball bunny hop on the schedule, and golfers were stacking up.

I suddenly realized I was as tired as I'd ever been. Hungry too and fragrant. Nova, for her part, was hanging awfully close and gazing at me with something other than devotion. She hadn't eaten either, so I decided to run home. We'd take an hour off, come back revived, and start searching all over again.

I suggested Agatha do the same, but she couldn't bring herself to leave, and Ethan was already back to wandering the surrounding woods by then. I promised myself I'd hurry back, and my Chevy did me the favor of starting. It looked like an ordinary morning in the country until I reached the Afton road. A couple of state policemen had choked the roadway down with their cruisers. They were handing out orange sheets of paper printed with a photo and a description of Hattie Womble. Her age. Her build. Her frail condition. The state of mind she might be in.

For a moment, it felt like we were all in this thing together in a decent, human sort of way. Then I noticed, driving down the mountain, lots of balled up orange trash, blowing along the roadway, caught up in the ditch.

Of course, I looked in the basement of the big house again. Still no Hattie. No Howard either. I went up to the barn as well, even climbed into the hay loft. Then me and Nova walked the pasture edge and peered into the pond.

We ate. All of us. The cat didn't appear to notice we'd been gone. Then I showered and changed my clothes, called Nova and went back out to the truck. I opened my driver's door, and she bounded past me and leaped inside. Standing there about to climb in myself, I could imagine my day before me. I'd go back up the mountain and try to be helpful at Evergreen. I'd probably end up searching where I'd searched already, pass my time consoling Ethan and Agatha, filling Captain Frank's hot water cup.

The captain had his team looking close and spiraling out and away. That was conventional and sensible of him and was sure to turn up Hattie in time by exhausting all the places she might be. Standing there at the truck I began to wonder if I couldn't better serve by doing everything the captain might think foolish and unproductive. His job was to recover Hattie Womble in any shape he might find her. I wanted to come across Ethan's grandmother while she was still okay. I still had various hunches I was tempted to act upon, so I decided me and Nova would go our own way and do our thing for a while. We'd balance out the captain's great good sense and professional deliberation with the sort of erratic and spontaneous running around he'd never get up to.

We stopped first at the Cavalier Mart at the bottom of Afton Mountain, and I quizzed everybody who pulled up to the pump islands for a while. Though I didn't turn up anyone who'd laid eyes on Hattie himself, I did find a woman who had a friend who'd mentioned to her in passing that he'd just about run an old lady down the evening before.

"Where?" I asked her.

She pointed nowhere much and shrugged.

"I need to know where exactly," I said.

She studied me, exasperated. Exactly is hardly something people specialize in around here.

"He didn't say," she told me.

"Can you call him?"

"Now!?"

I nodded. "It's important."

She reached in her car, and fished around in her handbag. She came out with her phone and called her friend. "There's some guy here," she said. "He wants to know about the woman you saw in the road."

"Silver hair?" I asked. "A sweater and a skirt?"

She got as far as "Silver . . ." before she handed me her phone. "Here." You would have thought I'd asked her to rotate my tires.

I just smiled. I'd learned that from Nova. I took her phone and said, "Hey."

Her friend had seen a woman who sounded like Hattie Womble. He'd come across her near twilight up where the parkway meets the Skyline Drive. That was a

heck of lot farther from Evergreen than we'd reasoned
she could get.

So I had to recalibrate my hunches and reconsider
Hattie's prospects. The chances seemed good to me she
was up in the park somewhere. There was a ranger
station, a snack bar, and a couple of roadside
campgrounds. She could have reached any of them by
now if she'd stayed on the road and walked through the
moonlit night.

I called Ethan and told him what I'd heard. It
proved the only morsel they had, and he tried to interest
Tad/Tod in it but didn't get anywhere. They'd done
quite a lot of vectoring, according to Tad/Tod, and that
portion of the park was well out of their perimeter.

"He says she couldn't get there," Ethan told me
after I'd listened in already through his phone.

"My guy saw her," I said. "Let's have a look. Why
don't you take the campgrounds, and me and Nova'll
poke around in the woods."

The truth is, it's hard to know what people will do
or where they might turn up. I'd been thinking of Hattie
as weak on her pins and more than a little halting, but I
almost always saw her just sitting in a chair. Though
she'd move around the Evergreen lawn a little, there was
hardly ever call for her to walk with vigor and purpose.
I'd just assumed she couldn't without much reason to
assume it.

So we left the Cavalier Mart, me and Nova, and
headed straight up the mountain. I turned up the ramp
on the ridge and headed north into the national park.
About a half mile shy of the gatehouse where you pay
the entrance fee, there's a parking lot that the bikers and
the hikers use. A path at the head of the lot leads
straight to the Appalachian Trail.

I left the road itself to Ethan, and me and Nova
struck out up the path. I didn't expect to meet hikers.
I'd seen general trail traffic fall off to next to nothing
over the years. You'd still run across the occasional
Maine to Georgia sort, but there were fewer of them
than there used to be and almost nobody out for a
couple of days of simple trailside camping. Those folks

had graduated to RVs with kitchenettes and satellite dishes, showers and toilets and beds. Most summer evenings at a campground, even deep in the national park, you couldn't hear the crickets and the nightjars for all the canned TV laughter.

I figured I'd take the AT north to where it crossed the Skyline Drive, turn there and work the horse trail down to the river bottom. Then I'd return to the ridge on the fire road straight through Jerusalem Gap, check in with Ethan and figure what to do from there.

Somehow Nova seemed to know this wasn't our usual sort of walk. She saw plenty of deer, but she didn't chase a one. She stayed twenty yards in front of me with her head up and her nose working. I called out for Hattie once or twice, but only crows answered back.

The trail was deserted and dusty. There wasn't much autumn in the air. We were probably three weeks from our first frost, and summer was hanging on. Even up on the ridge in the deep woods, it was hot and buggy this day. Uncommonly still and quiet.

We took a detour to check a shelter, more like a three-walled shed which didn't look to have seen any campers for a while. There was stale ash in the firebox and a few weathered scraps of trash. The spring -- down a rocky, stair-step path -- looked weedy and skimmed over.

We saw an adolescent bear up in an oak once we were back on the trail. We were on him before he could scamper down, and he bleated like a lamb for his mother. I could hear her chuffing somewhere too close by in the underbrush, and me and Nova put her behind us quicker than was dignified.

When we came to where the orange-blazed horse trail crossed, we took it down the eastern face of the mountain. It descended in gentle loops. I paused along the way, cupped my hands to my mouth and called out for Hattie Womble. This time I didn't even get so much as crows by way of reply. I was left to hope Ethan was having better luck at the campgrounds.

As we went farther down slope towards the river bed, I could hear the slow stream's anaemic trickle. It

got to where we weren't even spooking and driving much
wildlife anymore. The odd tree squirrel. Finches in the
leaf litter. The only snake we saw was dead, a harmless
ring-necked ground snake something had half eaten for
dinner.

When we reached the river, I walked straight across
it without even getting damp. Nova drank a little, and I
wished I'd carried something for us to eat. I perched on
a sycamore log, the one I'd used for a bridge when the
river was violent, and I allowed myself to feel just like I
had in the big house basement when I'd found out Hattie
Womble hadn't come to see the joists.

My phone had just enough of a signal to ring when
Ethan called me but not enough gain to let me hear what
he was trying to say. I thought he said he was in the
park, and maybe he told me he'd been to a campground.
Possibly he said he was fond of strawberries and
macaroons. Garbled squeaks and imagination were all I
had to go on. I tried to tell him where I was, but I didn't
have any faith he could hear me. Being down by the
Moorman River was like being in a hole in the ground,
so I decided it was time to forge ahead and gain the ridge
again.

It was still and hot down by the stream bed, but as
we ascended on the trail, a breeze found us as late
morning sunlight did as well. I was weary and moving
slow. Nova was ahead of me sniffing the air. I had to
watch for snakes and listen for bears and still search for
Hattie Womble while slogging along a weedy fire road
that ran straight up the mountain crease.

I was struggling to keep pace with the dog and
trying not to inhale gnats when I noticed the first of the
stone grave markers in among the scrub. Jerusalem Gap
didn't seem so glorious to me at that moment. It was
just on the way to the ridge line and my truck, so I wasn't
nearly as attentive as I had been earlier on the trail. But
even if I'd been on full alert, I doubt I would have seen
her.

Nova stopped in the fire road. She sniffed. She
shimmied. She glanced back at me and smiled. Then
she plunged off the road entirely and into a leafy thicket.

I figured she'd lost the thread a little and was back to chasing deer or rabbits or squirrels. When I reached the spot where she'd left the road, I called her, but she didn't budge. She was nose down among the plot of yellow orchids we'd seen before. Though droughty and withered a bit, they still looked arresting in their way.

"Come on, girl," I said and went back to watching for snakes. I'd covered ten yards before I realized she'd paid me no mind at all. "Nova!"

With that she picked up her head and looked at me. She barked one time and went back to what I could see now was licking. I entered the scrub and waded towards her, was almost upon her before I saw denim and white cotton, sky-blue cardigan wool. Nova was licking Hattie Womble's face. The woman looked to have collapsed in the orchids. I decided in an instant she'd marched all the way to Jerusalem Gap to expire.

She was pale and still. Though I might have been searching for her, she managed nonetheless to strike me as alarmingly out of place. Above ground in a spot with many dozens moldering below. I was already wondering how I'd tell Ethan when Hattie Womble giggled and laid her hand to Nova's head. Nova gave her a slow lick on the wrist and then looked over and smiled at me.

I reached them both in seconds.

"Oh, hey," was all Hattie told me.

"Hey yourself," I managed. "What in the world are you doing out here?"

"Out where?" she wanted to know. Then she caught sight of an orchid and touched it gently with her fingers. "Would you look at that."

I was little short of criminally unprepared to find her. I didn't have any food or water on me. Beyond Nova, I had no help. My phone was proving useless in the gap, and I'd brought no radio. I hated to imagine the dressing down Captain Frank L. Stenson would have given me.

When I tried to help Mrs. Womble up, she told me she was happy where she was. She looked like a woman who'd just awakened from surgery or a coma. She'd sit up a little with my help and lay immediately back down.

The only thing I could do was go for help, and since I'd yet to teach Nova Stay, I explained to Nova where I had to go and what I needed of her at that moment. She smiled at me and finally licked my hand as if to say, "Don't worry. I've got this, Dad."

I told Hattie Womble that I'd be right back with Ethan.

"How lovely," she said. She closed her eyes and laid her head back down with orchids for a pillow. I sure didn't want to bring her grandson back to find her dead on the ground.

"Lick her," I told Nova, and she did.

I had to go up that fire road harder and faster than I was fit for. I gave up on looking for rattlesnakes and just charged ahead full bore until the sweat was pouring off of me and my lungs were burning. I kept my phone in hand and glanced at it every twenty yards or so. I had no destination. I just needed to snag a signal. So I jogged up and out of the hollow and finally gained the ridge where my phone was just as useless to me as it had been down at the river. I ended up climbing a white oak, a majestic specimen with lower limbs as big around as my waist that reached almost to the ground.

So I walked up into the tree and just kept heading for the crown until I got two bars that came and went, depending on how I turned. I had to pose and twist and raise one arm to make a call go through. I was a regular spectacle with nobody to see me.

I got Ethan's voicemail. He was probably in a hollow too. "Found her," I said. "She's okay." Then I dug up Officer Crocker's number and called him as well. Partly for help in bringing Hattie Womble out of the gap. Partly because Eddie was geared to appreciate the wonder of a dog.

Eddie went and found Ethan. I met them at the top of the state road, where the maintenance ends and the rugged park takes over.

"What's she doing out here?" was the first thing Ethan rolled out of the car and said.

"Don't really know," I told him. "But you'll get to ask her yourself."

They hadn't called anybody just yet. That was Eddie being careful. He didn't want to report a live woman found until he'd seen her with his own eyes. I led them down the fire road and into Jerusalem Gap. With the scrub grown up and the markers hidden, it looked like almost any hollow until we got down to the woman and the orchids and the dog.

Nova had stretched out on the ground. We could see her head above the undergrowth as we approached. She'd turn and give Hattie Womble a long, slow collie lick when that struck Nova as just what she was needing.

Ethan charged ahead of us and went crashing through the scrub. Nova greeted him with a lick as well.

"You all right, Gom?"

I couldn't truly breathe again until I'd heard her voice. It was weak and frail, but she was no worse than I'd left her.

Me and Eddie left the fire road and joined them back in the brush. Eddie noticed the grave markers by tripping over a few.

"What is this?" he asked me.

"Cemetery," I told him. "Graves all through here and halfway down the hill."

Eddie squatted beside Mrs. Womble and all his police paraphernalia rattled and squeaked.

"Hey here," Eddie said to Mrs. Womble. "We've been looking for you."

She apologized for any trouble she might have caused us. She had an appetite, she told us, for pudding. The yellow kind they served at the dining hall. She thought it was custard. It came in a coffee cup.

"We'll get you some," Ethan promised her, "but first we've got to get out of here."

We didn't so much help her up as lift her clear off the ground. We set her back down on the fire road. She tried to walk a little, but she told us she was tired and hungry and a bit too sleepy to stand. So we carried her, me and Eddie mostly because we were about the same size and we'd soon found a way to bring her along between us. Ethan went up ahead and walked backwards mostly, offering encouragement to his Gom.

Eddie made a radio call once we'd gained the ridge.
He gave instructions for where the rescue squad should
meet us. We worked back along the ridge line to Eddie's
county cruiser and came down off the mountain with
me and Eddie up front. Hattie was flanked by Ethan
and Nova in back. Nova would lick her occasionally.
Nova would gaze out the window. Every now and again
I'd turn and Nova would look at me and smile.

We met the EMTs at the post office down in
Greenwood. The best thing they did for Hattie Womble
was give her a chocolate bar. It wasn't custard but it sure
did for her until custard could come along. She didn't
have any injuries. She wasn't even dirty. There were
orchids in her pockets, a tick on her neck. She'd scraped
her forearms on the prickly brambles in the gap.
Otherwise, she was fine and getting back to normal by
the minute.

When Ethan asked her why she'd wandered off, she
had an answer for him.

"Yesterday was my sister's birthday. I wanted
flowers for her."

"What sister?"

"Rosalie," Hattie Womble told him. "Prettiest hair
you've ever seen. Curly," she said, "and yellow, just like
these." She reached in her cardigan pocket and came out
with a pair of orchids. They were flattened and ratty
looking, but they were yellow all right.

When I looked at Ethan, he shook his head. He
didn't know about a sister. We both learned later from
his father that there'd been a Rosalie. She was taken by
fever, had died shy of two in 1929. Her birthday, as it
turned out, was in March.

Captain Frank L. Stenson conducted as impeccable
a news conference as you could ever hope to see. Tad/
Tod set him up with the valley spread behind him and
the sun blocked off so it wouldn't shine through Captain
Stenson's thinning hair. Douglas set up a map on an
easel and supplied the captain with a telescoping pointer.
Frank L. showed the assembled media -- three print
reporters and four TV correspondents -- how Mrs.
Womble left the grounds and where exactly she'd gone.

He didn't supply her reasons. He wasn't interested in those. It was easier on Captain Frank L. Stenson just to call Hattie Womble confused.

Dwight tried to dote on his mother, but he wasn't any good at it. Even slightly addled, she still remembered precisely who and what he was. Consequently, she backed him off, had a brief chat with his wife, and went inside to let the Evergreen doctor give her the once over.

"Mr. Prickly." I could tell Agatha was finally smiling again even before I'd turned around. She had a crushed orchid in her hand, a flattened one from Hattie Womble's cardigan pocket. "How on earth did she get way over there?" she asked me.

I was still a little amazed myself, though it was as close as the big house basement where I'd assumed I'd find her taking the timbers in. What could I do but shrug? "She must have really wanted to go."

"Come on, girl," I said to Nova, and she trailed me to the truck. She managed to jump into the cab, but only barely. I was feeling a little done in and creaky myself as I slipped in behind her. The engine fired, and Nova sprawled on the seat as we rolled off Afton Mountain. She grunted and pitched on her back. She slept with four feet in the air.

XIII

We threw a party in Nova's honor over at the big house. It was our every-other-Thursday get together, so it was regular lunch for us humans and a special Anguillan stew for Nova. Agatha had whipped up a meaty, bland concoction for the dog, something Nova could both savor and not gak up on the floor.

I told Ben and Billy and Agatha about my various Hattie searches -- up on the Blue Ridge Parkway, through the moonlit woods, down in the basement with Howard the blacksnake digesting behind the furnace. Then Jerusalem Gap. I still felt sure I would have missed Hattie Womble if Nova hadn't struck out through the scrub.

Nova had developed a slight limp. I figured she'd stepped on something in the woods, and she was a little off her feed and looking skinny to me. So I carried her into Walter who did that thing he always did. He felt around. He studied her. He wiped his hands on his pants. We left with all-purpose antibiotics in case some bug was working on her, and I told myself -- the way people will -- that she was doing fine.

I took Nova up to Evergreen after the dust had settled. Mrs. Womble had spent a couple of weeks as an unwilling celebrity prop. Once we'd found her and the authentic news stories about her had all played out, she'd get interviewed every now and again for how-to-tend-to-your-geezer features. She was even gracious about it for the first four or five occasions, but she finally got tired of being the white haired lady who'd wandered off, the one the writers talked to like she was three years old.

Arthur Bigelow did her the courtesy of chasing the final reporter away. He swatted the woman across the backside with his cane. "Go on with you," he told her as he cocked for a second blow.

Nova didn't tour the lawn at all but sat with Mrs.
Womble. Ethan showed up when school let out. We
didn't stay too long outside. It was the end of
September by then, and autumn was coming on in
earnest. Evergreen had suffered a little, had lost a
patient or two, but there wasn't too much of an uproar
since Hattie had turned up fine.

Looking back, I know Nova was sick by then, and
maybe I should have seen it. But she just kept smiling
and poking and licking and didn't limp in a regular way.
She didn't have much of an appetite. I just thought she
was getting picky. By my calculation, with the coming of
October, she was slightly older than a year. It seemed fit
and proper to me that she'd slow down at least a little, so
I didn't worry until she grew gimpy in a regular sort of
way.

It got to where she was flinging her left front paw
out before her as she walked. I let her outside one
morning and watched her wander around the yard. She
seemed happy enough and didn't appear to be in pain.
But I'd seen enough of her kind up at Evergreen. She
walked like she'd had a stroke.

For a week or so I treated her like I treat myself. We
finished up her antibiotics and waited for the trouble to
pass. I called Walter, and he told me to bring her in
whenever I could manage. He didn't seem too worried.

I got slowed down a little by Michael. The
McShanes had flown in for a weekend, and Michael had
decided he wanted a billiard room on what he called the
parlor floor. He meant upstairs in the space above the
foyer. They'd been calling it the sewing room, though I
can't say why exactly. Mrs. McShane would sooner
rebuild a transmission than sew. It turned out Michael
had seen a billiard table at a Baltimore antiques show, a
squat massive specimen that had come out of a harbor-
side pool hall. He'd bought it before he'd decided
exactly where it might end up.

So there was a refit for me to oversee, shelves to tear
out and a floor to replace, craftsmen to find for billiard
room touches like federalist cue racks and a Jeffersonian
beer tap. It was consuming as big house work went, so I

kind of let Nova go. I convinced myself her limp was probably canine sciatica. I'd had more than a few bouts with the stuff myself and had walked a little like her.

But then she started holding her head cocked, turned a little to the right, and the guy delivering Michael's billiard room stools glanced at Nova on his way into the house and asked me, "What's wrong with your dog?"

When Walter saw her limp into the examination room, he looked from her to me and just said, "Hmm." It was a grim one as Hmms go. I could tell he had dark thoughts.

I asked him, "What?"

Walter turned Nova on her back right there on the linoleum floor. "See this?" he said. Both of her eyes were twitching from side to side.

"Yeah."

"Nystagmus," Walter told me. I don't think I'd ever heard him use a proper medical word before.

Walter laid out his diagnosis for me. She had vestibular disease. If it was located in her ear canal, then he could probably treat it. But if she was limping around and twitching from a lesion on her brain, then there wasn't too much Walter could do in the long term.

I was thunderstruck. I dropped into a chair in the corner of the room. "I might lose her?"

Walter nodded.

"Well damn, Walter. Now I've gone and loved her like you said."

"Let's don't write her off just yet. She's pretty young for the ear canal kind, but you never know with stuff like this."

"What if I'd brought her in sooner?"

"Wouldn't have mattered," Walter told me.

Ever since, I've been ashamed that I was worried about myself.

Walter put her on stronger antibiotics, just in case she only had an infection, and he dosed her up on a powerful steroid in case it was cancer in her brain.

She got better for a couple of weeks. The limp went away, and her head hung straight, but, like I said before, I'm just not built to be optimistic. I waited for the limp to come back, and it did. The steroids only succeeded at slowing nature's course for a few weeks. She started flinging her foot. Her head cocked over. Nova wandered around in circles. Soon she didn't have the balance to even stand up in a regular way.

I'd help her. I'd hold her upright. I'd feed her out of my hand. We passed whole afternoons out in the sun-washed pasture. She'd lay on her side and gaze up at me, and the cows would approach as close as they dared to see what we were about.

It all happened so fast, I hardly had time to prepare myself to lose her.

I knew it couldn't go on, but I couldn't say when or how it would end. Agatha and Billy and Ben and Ethan all said their goodbyes to Nova, but I was selfish. I just couldn't let her go. I'd lift her onto my bed at night so she could sleep beside me. I had to hold her upright so she could drink her water, and I steadied her while she did her business. Every day she seemed to get a little weaker, and yet I still hung on.

I finally carried her with me to that horsy woman's estate up in the glen. She'd called for wood and had come out to show me, like usual, where to stack it.

Her whippets were running around the yard, chasing each other and playing.

"Where's that dog of yours?" she asked me. It felt like a needle in the heart.

"I left her at home," I told her. "She's feeling a little poorly."

I laid the woman's fire. I turned down her cocktail. I went back out to the truck.

Nova's feet were at the far door. Her head was near my lap so I could drive and glance down and she could look up at me.

"Hey," I said, like I always did these days when I got in.

She usually managed to give me a lick on my trouser leg. This day she didn't attempt it. She just looked at me in a way that said, "Today's as good as any."

Out on the ridge line proper at Afton, I went west instead of east. When the woman with the pile of hair at the clinic reception desk told me Walter was off that afternoon, I could have just gone home. But Nova wouldn't let me. She kept looking at me like she was keen to have me know she'd had enough.

We found Walter in his music shed. I was carrying Nova in my arms. Walter, of course, knew just what we were up to.

He had me come in and sit down for a minute with Nova on my lap. There was just the one chair, so I sat on the floor while Walter played his cello. He'd been working up a Bach sonata and had the prelude down. The one with all the sawing that even I had heard before. Walter was hardly concert ready, but for a guy in his back yard teaching himself the cello in a renovated tool shed, Walter sounded pretty all right to me.

"That was nice," I told him, once he'd almost hit the final note.

"Let's go then," was all he said to me and all he needed to say.

He took us in the back clinic door. Before I laid Nova on a table, Walter covered it for her comfort with a quilt.

She was getting my usual kiss on the snout when he gave her the first injection. A sedative just to put her under before a stronger one put her down. As she sank, she found my hand and gave me one last slow loving lick. Then Walter brought out the second syringe. He showed it to me. I nodded. She wheezed a little there at the end, and then she was just gone.

I remember removing her collar. I sort of remember Walter talking to me about when I could pick up the ashes, about how I'd done the right thing, about how awfully hard it was. He tried to usher me out the back door to avoid the reception ladies, but I marched right out to the counter so I could pay.

They were both there, the one with the hair and the regular one as well. The ancient cat on the counter swatted at me from his towel. Brady was over in the

waiting area terrorizing a beagle. They didn't know what
to charge me for, so I was the one who had to tell them.

The lady with the big hair came out from behind the
counter. She had dogs too. She gathered me in a
hug.

I'd gone in with a constant companion and come
out with just a collar. It was a staggering thing to realize,
and I lingered on the walk. I glanced over to find that
zebra pressed against the pasture fence. His head was
hanging over the top wire, and he was studying me hard.
He kept it up as I walked over to him.

I figured he'd wheel and run away. That's what he'd
always done, but he just stayed where he was and
whinnied like a regular, unstriped horse. I reached my
hand out, and that zebra let me rest it on his snout.

I didn't know exactly where to go or precisely what I
was doing. An empty truck was bad enough. An empty
house was sure to be worse. I ended up on the lawn at
Evergreen. The patients were all inside. The season for
sitting outdoors had passed, and they'd soon be packing
the Adirondack chairs back into the basement. I parked
myself by the Rose of Sharon bush which was leafless
branches now.

I didn't call for Agatha. She saw me through the
door light and came out. I didn't need to tell her a thing
since the sight of me said enough. I was sitting there
wearing Nova's orange collar like a bracelet.

We laid her to rest in Jerusalem Gap on a fine
November afternoon. I was joined in the woods by a few
of her friends, six of us together. Ben and Billy and
Ethan. Officer Eddie Crocker in his full dress uniform.
Agatha who, up until then, had only seen the place in a
dream.

Nova had come back to me in a cardboard box,
looking like a cup of grate ash. I had a few words I'd
planned to say, but I couldn't get them out. The scrub
had died away in the frost, so we could see all the grave
markers. We were gathered by the one where the yellow
orchids would sprout out in their glory come spring. I

seasoned the ground with Nova, and the boys laid a
wreath they'd made -- honeysuckle vines and Indian pipe,
bittersweet and purple asters -- all of them bound up
with Carl and Nova's weathered leather leash.

Ethan sang his grandmother's Jerusalem Gap song.
He'd turned up all the words somehow. Eddie had
carried his rifle down, and he fired off a full salute.

We hiked out and went down to Homer's Grill,
where I'd taken Nova that first day. We sat outside at a
picnic table, even though it was cool and breezy, and we
talked about my fine dog. We talked about Ethan's Gom.
I tried to come a little back to life.

XIV

My truck runs well now. I don't know why.
Everything I've tinkered with lately, I've tinkered with
before. It's the dry mountain air or the phase of the
moon or just dumb vehicular luck, but my Chevy never
fails to start and chugs along without a hiccup.

Michael is reconsidering his billiard room now that
it's complete. It turned out Michael has no knack for
pool and nobody to play it with. Everything else is
essentially the same. Pom Pom just keeps on going. We
all still get together for lunch and chat every other
Thursday. I visit Ethan and his grandmother a couple of
times a week, and I take Agatha to Staunton for dinner in
a regular sort of way. She usually calls me Donald now
instead of Mr. Prickly.

I cut firewood and split it and haul it. I read books
on my sofa since the cat continues to prefer my reading
chair. I've put Carl's bed away again. I've packed away
Nova's dishes. Her orange collar hangs from the prong
of a deer antler I found on a hike. It's tough to enter the
woods without her, difficult everywhere else as well. The
lady in the glen, in a bid to console me, tried to give me a
whippet. I settled for a cocktail instead.

I find myself haunting the stretch of road where
Nova got put. More times than I'd care to admit it, I'll
drift to the shoulder and stop. I'll raise my hood and
fiddle with a plug wire or a relay or just lounge against
the quarter panel and pass a half an hour.

You never know what might come your way if you
hang around to let it. That's a brand new way of
thinking for me. I learned it from a dog.